Ann Summers

Lust and Longing
Erotic Tales from Madame B

Ann Summers

Lust and Longing
Erotic Tales from Madame B

EBURY
PRESS

1 3 5 7 9 10 8 6 4 2

Published in 2008 by Ebury Press, an imprint of Ebury Publishing

A Random House Group Company

Text written by Siobhan Kelly © Ebury Press 2008

The Random House Group Limited Reg. No. 954009

Addresses for companies within the Random House Group can be found at
www.randomhouse.co.uk

A CIP catalogue record for this book is available from the British Library

The Random House Group Limited supports The Forest Stewardship
Council (FSC), the leading international forest certification organisation.
All our titles that are printed on Greenpeace approved FSC certified
paper carry the FSC logo. Our paper procurement policy can be found at
www.rbooks.co.uk/environment

Mixed Sources
Product group from well-managed
forests and other controlled sources
www.fsc.org Cert no. TT-COC-2139
© 1996 Forest Stewardship Council

To buy books by your favourite authors and register for offers visit
www.rbooks.co.uk

Typeset by Palimpsest Book Production Limited,
Grangemouth, Stirlingshire

Printed and bound in Great Britain by
CPI Cox & Wyman, Reading RG1 8EX

ISBN: 9780091926434

Welcome to the second instalment of Madame B's full-length erotic adventures.

Lust and Longing explores themes of control and surrender as seen through the eyes of Jenna, a young woman who found that, when it comes to sex, you can't always get what you want, but sometimes you might get what – or who – you need.

I travel the world collecting true stories of sex and seduction: women confide in me, and I write everything down in my red leather journal. My favourite stories, the most sexy and inspirational confessions, are the ones I publish.

Jenna's story is one of my favourites: her adventure spanned the world and involved money, power, lust and indulgence — all fabulous ingredients for a life lived to its limits. Jenna was obsessed with power, both in the bedroom and the boardroom. But when she met Alexander, this dynamic, decadent dominatrix found that sometimes it's good to receive as well as to give.

I hope that Jenna's story inspires you to step out of your usual sexual role and push your limits. The potential rewards are orgasmic!

Happy reading,
Love,

Madame B x

CHAPTER ONE

Jenna was 17 when she had her first taste of power. It was a hot December day, perfect rollerblading weather, and she was soaking up the Sydney heat in her bikini top and a pair of cut-off denims. She skated figure eights on the smooth pavements of Circular Quay, aware of but not acknowledging the admiring glances she and her friends drew from tourists and commuters on the ferries that pulled in and out of the harbour. Jenna loved the freedom that her blades gave her, and soon skated away from her friends and around the other side of the quay to the Opera House, whose white roofs bounced the sunshine back onto Jenna's bronzed skin.

Cocky, over-confident, she tried skating with her hands behind her back, skating backwards, taking corners with her eyes closed, zipping in and out of the sweeping nooks and alcoves of this unique building. Dangerously close to the curved edge of the Opera House, Jenna raised her left leg a little and wheeled around into a blind spot. She smacked into a strange man, making full body-to-body contact. He was dressed as conservatively as Jenna was casual, and she felt the buttons of his shirt and the stiff silk of his tie against her nearly naked torso. She also had time to register a broad, muscular body and flat stomach. Her blades added inches to her height, so she was around six feet tall: she was at eye level with this guy and she could feel something else too, even for the split second she was there, a hardening in the crotch that was level with her thigh. As she pushed herself back, disentangled her long, dark, sea-salt and wind-ruffled hair from his shoulders, she looked him in the eye. He was younger than she'd thought, only in his early twenties, despite the clothes that were designed for a man twice that age. He was a hottie, she realised, with a square jaw and hazel eyes framed by thick, light-brown hair which curled a little in the heat.

But it wasn't his looks that were stirring a new and overwhelming feeling in Jenna. It was the look in his eyes. A potent combination of both panic and arousal. She was young, he knew she knew he had a hard-on, he was still half-entangled in public with a semi-naked teenager and he was clearly freaked out as well as horny. This gave Jenna a taste of something new, delicious and addictive: power. This man was at her mercy. And she liked it.

A pulse began to hammer between her legs and she was conscious of goosebumps developing on her golden skin and her nipples stiffening as if they were cold, even though the sun was beating down on her. Something primal, something programmed deep into her before she was born, made her speak. Although she had never uttered words like these aloud before, she felt as though she were finding her voice for the very first time.

'Is your prick hard?' she asked, raising an eyebrow, a rhetorical question since the bulge in the guy's trousers was all the evidence she needed. He gulped and nodded. The prick in question swelled again behind tailored linen.

'Get it out.' He shook his head. Jenna put her hands on her hips, stuck out her tits, enjoying his total lack of control over his body.

'I can't.'

'Get it out. I want to see it. I've never seen one before.' This was only half true. Jenna had plenty of experience, fumbles in the dark with high-school boyfriends, and she knew what it felt like to have a dick in her, to hold one in her hand, although she had never felt inclined to examine one at close quarters. She had wondered, at those times, what all the fuss was about. But this feeling of power over a total stranger was provoking urgent, hot changes in her body which were new and welcome: this, she suddenly knew, was the buzz people were talking about.

'I'm not asking, I'm telling,' said Jenna, discovering to her delight that the bossier she got, the more intense this warm wet feeling between her legs grew. 'Take your right

hand, undo your fly, and take your dick out of the trousers.'
Glancing around to check they could not be seen, the guy
did as Jenna told him. His hand was shaking as he fumbled
with his belt buckle and unzipped himself. Jenna admired
the sturdy, peach-coloured stick of flesh that continued to
grow before her eyes, watching appreciatively as the angle
of his hard-on grew smaller until it was bolt upright,
almost touching his belly.

His trousers rode down around his hips, creeping
further towards his knees. He could not have run away
even if he wanted to. This further emboldened Jenna.

'Stroke it,' she said. 'Make it bigger for me.'
Whimpering and shaking his head, the man appeared to
refuse, but his dilated pupils and an erection that still
seemed to be swelling and rising told another story. The
stranger in the suit brought his hand to his dick, making
a loose fist and wrapping his fingers over the head of his
penis, pulling back the foreskin to reveal a proud, round
helmet. A droplet of clear juice glistened on the very tip,
and Jenna bent down to examine it further. She was so
close that her breath caressed his skin, and she observed
as another tiny trickle of liquid emerged from the tip of
his cock. I did that, she thought, and when she stood
upright again, she was surprised to find that she had slid
her hand underneath her bikini top without realising it,
and her fingertips were making circles around her swelling

nipples. She pinched her breast, to clarify her thoughts as well as to increase her arousal.

She locked eyes with him and felt herself grow wetter. She had never seen an expression like it. The mixture of fear and desire left no doubt that he was enjoying himself as much as Jenna herself – was just as excited by this sudden, random, horny encounter as she was. The difference was, she was the one in control.

'It's good,' she murmured in a low whisper and casting a glance of mock disgust at his perfect prick, 'but I think it could get bigger.' Now it was his turn to speak.

'Please . . . oh, this is torture,' he cried, and she realised for the first time that he was not Australian: his accent was British, more clipped and distinct than hers. His voice carried years of history and discipline and good schooling: Jenna thought of him in a school uniform like the boys from the privileged public schools she'd read about, and the wetness between her legs warmed the gusset of her panties.

'Please,' he was saying, 'just touch me, you don't have to take it in your mouth, just put your hand on it.'

Jenna shook her head, glanced over her shoulder to make sure they were still alone and skated a sweeping circle around the guy. The only part of herself she allowed to touch him were dark tendrils of hair blowing across his face like dozens of tiny whips. He reached out to touch her, but she was too quick for him. She skated backwards out of his reach. Somehow, she knew he wouldn't move. Slowly, deliberately, she raised her hands above her head and executed a perfect twirl in front of him, letting her shorts ride up so that he could see the line where her legs joined her ass, stretching her arms so that her bikini top rode up, displaying the underside of her breast, threatening to reveal her nipple but not quite doing so. As she lowered her arms and pressed them together to deepen her cleavage, the guy's hand moved faster and faster over his twitching dick.

'Slow down,' said Jenna. 'It's not over till I say so.' Where the hell were these words coming from? She'd never heard people speak to each other like that before, but she felt as though she were reading from a script that was written down somewhere in the back of her mind. And saying them felt good. Especially when he bowed his head and murmured something that sounded like, 'Yes, mistress.'

Instinctively Jenna knew that there was a delicate art to what she was trying to do. Overdo it, and he would come before she gave him permission to. Be too lenient with him, and she would lose the authority that was getting them both off so much. Arching and twisting her young body so that he was visually stimulated while he wanked, she watched his face for signs of surrender. When she thought he was about to reach the point of no return, she acted. With a simple flick of a ribbon, Jenna released the halterneck of her bikini top so that her breasts were exposed. First one breast then the other was on show but stayed firm and pert without the support of the bra, two perfect teardrops topped by pinky-brown nipples that seemed to point up towards the sky.

'Now,' she said, watching the guy's face crumple like a ball of paper as he came, his features contorted as his dick bounced and twitched, sending a jet of warm white liquid into the air, some of it landing on Jenna's breasts. After his five seconds of ecstasy had subsided, his face became smooth and unlined again, as though someone had unscrewed the paper and returned it to its virgin state. Jenna thought, as she fastened her bikini and covered her breasts again, that she had never really known somebody look quite so at peace and content. Or so beautiful. Seconds after that, panic of quite a different kind returned as he realised that he had just shot his load over a complete stranger, and that somehow she had made him do it. He began to stammer an explanation.

'I'm terribly sorry, I don't know what came over me . . .'

'I think you'll find that you're the one that came over me,' said Jenna with a wink. 'Go on, fuck off out of here.' The suited stranger obeyed this final order with haste, tucking his still-swollen dick back into his trousers, post-cum dribbles already staining the fabric on the inside of his thigh. He disappeared around the corner of the curved building, and was gone.

Jenna leaned back on the sun-warmed white tiles of the Opera House. She could not think at all, she could only feel. Her tits felt heavy and tender, her pussy so swollen and sensitive that it hurt when she closed her legs and her whole body felt as though it was in motion. From a distance, an observer would have assumed that the lone teenage girl rocking backwards and forwards was moving in time to a song played through headphones. They could not have known that she was squeezing her thighs together, letting her pussy lips massage her clitoris, until the roaring in her ears subsided and juices flooded her shorts as she succumbed to her first orgasm, while the image of the anonymous stranger's helpless, beautiful face danced before her eyes.

CHAPTER TWO

The gap between finding out what turned her on and finding similar souls with the same tastes was a short one. She plucked up the courage to walk into a sex shop in Oxford Street and picked up a couple of magazines and flyers with pictures of the kind of woman she wanted to become: PVC-clad, or whip-wielding women in fabulous, skin-tight outfits who radiated confidence, fun, and adventurousness – but most importantly of all, power. These women were unafraid to meet the camera's gaze, their defiant, heavily made-up eyes inviting her into their world. She was so nervous that she could barely meet the shop assistant's eye and shuffled out with the stack of magazines and flyers tucked underneath her arm, which she slipped inside a copy of the *Sydney Morning Herald*. Back home in her bedroom, she opened the cover of the first magazine, and what she saw aroused her so much so quickly that a little damp patch appeared on her panties before the page was even fully turned. It was a picture of a woman dressed in a metallic catsuit, the tips of her tits poking through slashes in the fabric. She was feeding a bulbous nipple to a naked and blindfolded man who knelt before her. Jenna's fingers found their way to the nub of her clitoris, her thumb stroking the tiny bud while forefingers made themselves into a tiny penis and jabbed in and out of her slippery slit. From first seeing the photograph to the moment she had an orgasm probably took about 15 seconds. She was hooked.

For two weeks, Jenna locked herself in her room, reading the magazines from cover to cover, absorbing every picture, touching herself as she read. She liked to read them sitting cross-legged, naked but for the only pair of high-heeled shoes she owned, one hand squeezing and pinching her tits, rolling her nipples between thumb and forefinger while the other hand flicked and rubbed at her clit. She used the paperclips that bound her college essays to clamp her nipples so that they felt numb – and then super-alive when she tore them off again. She fucked herself with the handle of her hairbrush, astonished at how wet she could get time after time after time.

She absorbed everything, words as well as images, learning that there was an entire parallel universe where people went to play games of power and submission, restraint and bondage. She learned that some women were naturally submissive, and loved to be dominated by men who played at being merciless, unflinching masters, while other women only felt true sexual gratification if they were the ones wielding all the power, who love to bring men to their knees, and command orgasms. No prizes for guessing which camp Jenna fell into. She was happy to find that if you were a woman submissive, also known as the sub, or a bottom, there were plenty of willing masters (or mistresses; many women enjoyed being dominated by other women), but that if you were a dominatrix, or a dom, or a top, then the supply of men willing to put their sexuality in your hands is almost limitless. Jenna knew that just reading the magazines was not enough. She had to go to one of these clubs, find these people, and become one of them. She laid the flyers on her bed like a deck of tarot cards and selected the one with the image she liked the most – a man's naked back decorated with a lattice-work of whip marks.

Jenna dressed for her first night wearing her usual denim cut-offs teamed with the high-heeled shoes which she wore daily when she spent hours bringing herself to orgasm, and a corset that she had found in a charity shop which cinched her athletic torso into an hourglass shape. She ringed her eyes with dark kohl and shook out her hair so that it became a wild, dark mane. Posing in front of her bedroom mirror, she had felt powerful and confident, but as she approached the entrance to the club, she began to feel nervous. What if her jean shorts made her look like a novice? Would anyone laugh at her? Would she be allowed to play the dominatrix on her first night – would anyone even let her watch, see how it was done?

She stood outside the location on the flyer, a doorway in a side street lined with office blocks on the south side of Sydney, hardly an area you would associate with deviant sexual activity. After inhaling and exhaling deeply, she pushed her way through and stepped into her new world for the first time.

The black-walled club was only a few square metres wide, and the dancefloor little bigger than her bathroom at home, but it was rammed with people she instantly recognised as kindred spirits. She could smell the rubber, leather and plastic of the clothes people wore here. Black shiny substances abounded, as did human flesh. Jenna had never seen so much skin displayed in so many different ways, so many pairs of trousers with cut-outs for the buttocks, crotchless panties, peephole bras . . . all the exotic finery she had seen in her magazines was suddenly paraded before her in a live fashion show. People were friendly and said hello, but she was intrigued to realise that although the whole point of the club was for sexual expression, she actually felt less leered at and hit upon than she would in an average city-centre bar.

As she nursed her drink, a Jack Daniels and coke, a girl not much older than Jenna with a shaved head, multiple piercings in her ears and wearing only a single length of black tape wound around her slim frame, smiled at her.

'You're new here, aren't you?' said this entrancing creature in a strong New Zealand accent. Jenna could only nod shyly. 'I'd recognise that look anywhere. I've only been coming here for about six months myself, and the first time I came in I was so nervous I hid behind a curtain in the first hour and a half. But I'll save you the trouble of doing that. It's a great crowd – let me introduce you to some people.' She pointed to a booth in the corner where a collection of bodies were drinking and laughing, draped over each other. They didn't stay still long enough for Jenna to count them, but she guessed there were six or so people, all young, all beautiful, all barely dressed. The sight of their bodies pressed up against each other and limbs casually intertwined almost made Jenna lose her breath. She shrugged off her uncharacteristic shyness.

'Sure, that would be great. I'm Jenna, by the way.' The shaven-headed girl held out her hand and Jenna shook it.

'I'm Kristin,' said her new friend, interlacing her fingers through Jenna's and leading her over to the corner booth. 'Come and meet the gang.'

The others turned out to be fellow students of Kristin's from the University of Sydney. Jenna was drawn to one of the guys, Mark, although she couldn't have said why.

He was not exceptional-looking, and his vest and jeans outfit was positively conservative compared to his friends' clothes. But there was a vulnerability about him which attracted her. Jenna liked the way he kept pushing his glasses further up his nose as they kept falling down, and the way his quiff was wilting in the heat of the club. Conversation flitted between talking about their university course, intriguing gossip about people Jenna didn't know and, of course, sex. Eventually, as she had known they would, they asked her what she was into.

'So, Jenna,' said Kristin. 'What brings a nice girl like you to a place like this?'

'Curiosity, I guess,' said Jenna.

'Well, of course,' said Kristin. 'Curiosity took me to all the interesting places I've been. What I meant was, what's your kink? We'll go first if you like. Me, for example, I've got a thing about rubber, can't help it, I just love the stuff, whether I'm wearing it or somebody else is. Then Anthony over there –' She pointed to a surfer-type guy with long hair and ripped muscles '– he's into watersports, both giving and receiving. Kerry here likes it up the arse. Jodie and Mark used to go out for a while but they're the world's worst couple; they both want to be dominated. Can you imagine? *Both* of them wanting to be sat on and abused? They never got anywhere!'

Laughter broke the tension while Mark smiled shyly.

Jenna knew now why she had felt drawn to him: she'd read that a good dom can always recognise a sub and vice versa. She had not believed it then but she believed it now. She pictured herself kneeling either side of Mark's thighs, pumping his stiff cock in her fist but forbidding him to come. She shivered, despite the sultry atmosphere in the club. Then she realised that the laughter had died down and that everybody was looking expectantly at her for an answer. She thought about saying, 'I think I might be a dominatrix,' but realised how feeble that would sound, because she *knew* she was, she just didn't have the experience. And experience was exactly what she was out to get.

'I'm a dom,' she announced to the group. Mark turned to Jodie.

'I told you,' he said to her, while Jodie shrugged. So Mark had recognised her, too. This night was only getting better.

As the night wore on, people began to drift away to find people to play with. Kristin took to the dancefloor with a man in a rubber suit who held her close, while Anthony disappeared to the bathroom with a stunning blonde on his arm and a wicked smirk on his lips. Kerry's eyes were glazed as she sat at the bar, a man's hand travelling over her ass, while Jodie was dancing in a group of friends.

It was just Jenna and Mark left alone. She knew what she had to do – but how to do it?

'I'm going for a walk around the club. I haven't explored properly yet. Want to come?' She kicked herself as soon as the words were out of her mouth. She should not have asked him if he wanted to come, she should have told him he was. And this was his territory, which put her at a disadvantage: she should have been the one to lead him around. But she noticed that when they got up to explore the warren of corridors and private rooms that comprised the club, he was happy to let her walk in front. Jenna soon found out that the place was much more extensive than she had first thought: as well as the main room, there were several velvet-lined chambers where couples could retreat to play with a little more privacy. Jenna felt her body throb from head to toe as she witnessed a man lying prone on a wooden rack while another man bent over him with a lit, dripping candle, carefully sending dribbles of hot wax everywhere but his raging, bulging cock.

Jenna soon found a deserted alcove where she and Mark could be alone. It was a small, purple nook with a curtained doorway. A black, wrought-iron candelabra hung from the ceiling. Real candles were wedged into its holes, and wax dripped onto the bed that dominated the centre of the room. It was upholstered in some kind of strange shiny fabric. Jenna ran her hand over it and realised it was plastic, enjoying the squeaks her fingertips made on it. Her heart began to race and her clitoris thrummed as she noticed shackles for wrists and ankles at the head and foot of the bed. She imagined Mark lying there, his body splayed like a starfish, and felt a swell of empowerment as she realised how easy it would be to make that vision a reality. Jenna's nipples began to harden, her clit swelling and pounding, and she was aware of the sound of her own breath. Then she realised it was not *her* breathing she could hear but that of Mark's, inches away from her, and the sweat on his brow and the rasping of his breath told her that now was the moment to strike. Jenna got behind Mark and grabbed both of his wrists. She noticed a small gold earring looping around his left earlobe and bit down on it, tugging it with her teeth and tongue before whispering in a stern voice that was not her usual tone:

'When I let go of you, you're going to take all your clothes off. You're going to be hard, and you're going to want to touch yourself, but you're not allowed to. I won't let you. You're going to put your hands in the air and spread your legs.'

Mark nodded and she heard him gulp. Obediently he raised his arms over his head and pulled off his vest to reveal a surprisingly muscular back. His glasses became entangled in his vest and he scrambled to retrieve them.

When he put them back on they were crooked. Jenna noticed that the skin on his back was criss-crossed with fading scars; obviously this boy was no stranger to the whip. Good to know. Mark unbuckled his belt, his breathing growing more audible by the second, and eased his jeans over his hips. His arse was high, round and defined and his legs were stocky and hairy. She liked his solid bulk: it was so much more exciting to dominate a well-built man than her physical inferior.

'Lie down on the bed.'

Mark knelt on all fours before rolling over onto his back like an obedient puppy on his first day of training. Jenna watched as his cock and balls rose in the air. He was young and virile and his hard-on kept rising until the tip of his dick obscured his navel. Jenna had to fight the urge to rip her own clothes off, straddle him and ride out that big hard cock until both of them came. But she couldn't, not yet, not yet.

The bed might as well have been custom-made to host Mark's young body. The restraints, which snapped shut like animal traps, were perfectly positioned to bind his wrists and ankles. They were made of coated steel, and Jenna felt her pussy pound as she imagined the red marks they would leave on him. She stood over him, thighs apart, hands on hips, licking her lips and wondering what to do with him next. The adrenaline coursed through her veins, as she realised that this was the first time she was finally putting into practice the dominatrix that she became when she practised in front of her bedroom mirror.

She began to prowl around the bed, examining Mark's body from every angle. Really, he was a fine example of the male species. The dark hair on his chest made a crucifix pattern and ran like a fuse wire down to his swollen prick. It wasn't the largest erection in the world, but it was one of the most perfectly formed. The skin on his penis was the same butterscotch colour as the rest of his body, but darkened as it became engorged with blood. A tiny mole on one of his symmetrical balls made him seem even more vulnerable, which increased Jenna's feelings of power.

'Call that a hard-on?' sneered Jenna, standing at the head of the bed and looking down at Mark. Her harsh words affected his prick like a massage: it grew an inch before her eyes, and finally the purple tip released itself from the foreskin. 'That's more like it,' said Jenna. 'Now, I wonder what to do with you?'

'Please, Jenna, please touch it,' whimpered Mark, closing his eyes. 'Put your hands on me.'

'In here, my name is not Jenna. You are permitted only to call me Mistress. And no, I won't touch it. You don't deserve my hands on your cock. My smooth hands running up and down your prick? Don't make me laugh.'

As she spoke, Jenna continued to pace around the

bed, Mark's eyes boring into her like lasers. He twisted his head; tried to angle his whole body so that he could have full view of her at all times. Jenna was trying desperately to stay in control of her own body as well as retain her command of Mark's. She was glad that she had worn her denim hotpants because the thick, roughly sewn seam of the crotch and the cold metal bulk of the buttons put deliciously agonising pressure on her clitoris with every step that she took. She turned her stride into a sashay, rubbing her thighs together and rolling her hips for maximum stimulation. At this rate, she too would experience a hands-free climax.

'I'm sorry, Mistress,' said Mark, his whole body shaking with frustration. 'What are you going to do with me?' Jenna looked down at the beautiful, helpless young man and realised that the greatest punishment she could give him was to withhold her touch.

'What do you want me to do?' she asked, arching an eyebrow.

'Oh God, I want you to do everything to me. I want to see your tits. Want you to bend over me so that they're in my face while you pull my prick so hard it's almost too painful to bear, and I want you to milk every drop of spunk from my body, and I want you to slap me around the face with your nipples. I want you to sit on my face, I want to taste your pussy, I want everything that could possibly happen while I'm tied up like this to happen between us. That's what I want, but Mistress, you've got me so horny that just a touch of your skin on mine will make me come.'

Jenna had not expected such a detailed reply, but by telling her what he did want, she knew how to torture him even more. She would give him none of the things he mentioned. She did not unfasten her corset, even though she knew her tits would look absolutely resplendent: she could feel her hardening nipples under the stiff boning. Although she wanted to feel the soft skin of his hard cock in her palms, she didn't do that. Although sitting on his face and smothering him would have given her the climax she too so greatly desired, she didn't do that. Instead, in her impossibly high heels, she elegantly got up onto the bed, looked down at Mark and then sat, cross-legged, between his legs. She could feel the heat from his body warming her own thighs. They were almost touching, and she could smell the sweet, salty tang of the fresh sweat that poured down on Mark's chest between his nipples.

'I wouldn't give you the satisfaction,' she said. 'This is my kind of bondage. It's all about withholding pleasure, Mark. I know you want to come. I know you want me to grab your prick and milk it, suck every drop of spunk out of you. You want me to wring it between my hands like a wet dishcloth until there's nothing left in those beautiful balls.' These vivid descriptions were having exactly the desired effect. Marks balls began to tense and rise up into his body and Jenna knew that the slightest touch would bring him to orgasm. 'But what you'd really like, Mark, is to fuck my tits, wouldn't you?' Mark closed his eyes and nodded. His body was in such delicious agony that he could not even speak any more. 'You want to know what colour my nipples are. Whether they're round or pointy. You want to look at my tits, as I push together, one on either side of your prick.' Mark looked as though he was close to tears. 'Forget it. It's not gonna happen. You don't deserve to see my tits.'

'Please, I need to come, I'm gonna come, help me, please . . .'

Jenna loved Mark's begging. She would have liked to prolong his agony, but she was not an experienced enough dominatrix to control her own orgasm, and Mark was not the only one fighting climax. She felt a dizziness take over her body as the pulse between her legs became a rapid fluttering. Hoping that Mark would not notice what she was doing, she hooked her thumb through the belt loops of her shorts and pulled the denim closer to her body, and rocked ever so slightly so that her clitoris was receiving the direct stimulation she craved. She began to relax as the pre-climax contractions built up in her pelvis. At the same time, she leaned down towards Mark's cock and blew gently on the spot where his balls and his cock met. He had begged her to be rough and manhandle him, but her warm breath travelling up and down the length of his dick was all it took for Mark to come, his body bucking and rising, his hips shooting up as his prick squirted out an arc of white spunk which sprayed over his belly and decorated it in lacy white patterns. His hips jerked up so fast and so quickly, that for a second Jenna thought he might even break the bonds which tied him to the bed. She could see that the extra restraint made his orgasm all the more intense.

And then she came too, while Mark was lost in his orgasm, biting her lip and trying to keep a straight face so that he would not see the contortions that twisted her expression.

Trying not to hurt her sensitive, swollen clit, Jenna reached down beside the bed and picked up Mark's discarded vest top. She used it to clean up the semen which he had squirted all over his body. It had pooled in his navel and Jenna used the cotton garment to gently mop it up. Tenderly she traced the trail of liquid that dotted his chest hair in pearls and mopped the tip of his cock. Then she held the vest to her nose and inhaled deeply, breathing in the delicious, unmistakable smell of a man's essence, and revelling in the fact that she had teased and tortured it out of his body.

After a couple of minutes, Mark recovered sufficiently

to open his eyes. He beamed up at her with a look of adoration that melted Jenna's heart and sent a fresh fizz of excitement to her clit. Nobody had ever looked at her like that before, but she knew she would see it again and again. She smiled back and tiptoed around his bed, gently unfastening the shackles that bound him there for the duration of their game. She had the last word before she left him.

'If that's what I can do with no hands,' she whispered into his ear, 'imagine what it will be like when I finally let you fuck me.' She turned on her heel and stalked out of the room, not giving him a backward glance.

On the other side of the curtain, in the corridor, Jenna saw Jodie, who was leaning against the wall, eyes closed, dress hitched up around her waist, hands down her panties. Through the blue silk, Jenna could see Jodie's fingers working, drumming on her clitoris. Jenna was fascinated; she had never seen another woman's face as she came and she could tell by Jodie's rapturous expression she was only seconds away. Sure enough, Jodie's knuckles tensed under her panties, her knees shook and bent and then her whole body relaxed and a dark flush spread across her face and chest. Despite her recent orgasm, Jenna found herself getting wet again. Jodie opened her eyes, and looked right at Jenna.

'I was watching you in there,' said Jodie in a voice

that was little more than a whisper. 'What you did with Mark. That was amazing. I nearly came without touching myself too, but I had to come outside and get myself off or you would know I was there.' Jenna wished she had known that she was being spied on: it would have made the experience even more intense and thrilling. Obeying a silent command in her own head, she grabbed Jodie's hands from her panties, and held the fingers up to her nose. I did that, too, thought Jenna, and for the first time, she wondered what it would be like to dominate another woman. She pushed Jodie against the wall, held her hands lightly around her neck and gave her an intense kiss that bordered on violent, forcing her bare knee between Jodie's legs and grinding her pussy against her soft thigh. She held Jodie's hands down by her sides, rubbing her clit up and down until she came again, this second orgasm a softer, subtler echo of the one that she had experienced just moments before. She drew away from the astonished, trembling Jodie, delivered a gentle bite to her soft cheek and walked down the corridor.

I walked in here a fetish virgin, thought Jenna, as she left the club, and I came out a bisexual dominatrix with two willing slaves at my beck and call. All in all, a good night.

Jenna's circle of fetish friends grew over the next three years, as did her wardrobe of outrageous outfits. She stayed in Sydney to go to university and continued her sexual education by night in the city's underground bars and clubs, until her reputation as the strictest, sexiest, most hard-bodied dom in Australia was cemented. Club and private work meant that student poverty was never an issue for Jenna, and she had more devoted slaves than she could find time to dominate, although she always kept a soft spot for Mark and Jodie.

And yet something was missing. Playing with like-minded friends in a permissive, consensual environment was delicious. But she had still never matched the thrill of that first, spontaneous exchange with the stranger in a suit whose name she had never known but who had been the first to bring out the dominatrix in her. She couldn't put her finger on it. There was no challenge, no risk, no danger dominating men and women who came to the club desperate to be whipped and bound. The challenge was to find a man, a real man, a hard and powerful man and break him – in the real world.

The turning point came one night at a private party in the suburbs. Jenna met Hugo, an impossibly polite Englishman who begged her to cane him to the point of orgasm. Jenna was only too happy to oblige, and after his lashing the two of them got chatting on the sofa.

'Your accent is so very charming,' he said and then,

taking in Jenna's flawless, gym-honed body, 'And you have a stunning figure, too. Really first-class.'

'I'm not the one with the accent,' she said, giggling at his old-fashioned vocabulary. 'I'll let you into a secret. Nothing makes me wetter than dominating a man with an upper-class-sounding voice like yours. I think it's all those centuries of money and power.'

'Ah, you should come to my part of the world,' he said. 'England is crawling with ex-public schoolboys just desperate for a good dominatrix. Biggest concentration of subs in the world, I'd say. Politicians – they're a rum bunch. Kinkiest bastards on the planet probably work in Westminster.'

Hugo didn't know it, but his casually uttered words were to change Jenna's life. Without ever having been to London, Jenna decided that that was where her future lay. The next morning she went into college and changed her course to sociology and politics. Over the next few months, she filled in a million application forms, applied for a thousand grants, spent an interminable summer working as an intern at the Australian parliament in Canberra where, despite exhaustive efforts, she couldn't find a fetish scene, and eventually got herself an interview as a research assistant for a junior minister in the House of Commons in London.

Jenna booked her flight, went shopping for a new

wardrobe and found an English friend of Kristin's whose flat she could crash in for a couple of days. On the flight from Sydney to the UK, she could barely contain her excitement. London – and its well-bred, well-spoken, powerful, rich and deviant men – weren't going to know what had hit them.

CHAPTER THREE

Kristin's friend Jacqueline had appointed herself tour guide and chauffeur as well as hostess for the first few days of Jenna's trip. A small, tidy-figured redhead in casual clothes and with artfully tousled hair, she met Jenna off her flight and drove her straight back to her East London flat, where Jenna collapsed on the futon and stayed asleep for ten hours. When she woke up, dozy and confused at nine in the evening, Jenna found Jacqueline dressed for a night out. It was quite a transformation – only the red hair convinced Jenna that this was the same dishevelled urchin who had picked her up from the airport earlier that day. With her hair set in pin curls, and the jaunty little pillbox hat on her head, a pencil skirt and high-heel combo that looked impossible to walk in, and a crisp white shirt underneath a dramatic red corset, Jacqueline looked every inch the burlesque scene queen.

'Wanna come out and play?' said Jacqueline. Her broad Cockney accent was very different to the clipped vowels of the Englishmen Jenna had met in Sydney, but equally charming. Jenna had to fight hard the temptation to say yes: she only had around 12 hours before her interview. For once her ambition overrode her desire to go out and play.

'Just this once, I'm going to have to say no,' she said. 'I really can't afford not to get this job tomorrow, and I just know that if I go clubbing, I'll get myself into all sorts of messy, dirty adventures and I won't want to go home until six o'clock in the morning.'

Jacqueline laughed, a pretty little gurgle that Jenna found surprisingly arousing. The dainty little woman was not Jenna's usual type at all. Jenna briefly closed her eyes, and allowed herself a mental vision of Jacqueline bound at the wrists and ankles, her slender young body lightly branded with the leathery lashes of Jenna's favourite whip. It quickened her pulse. Perhaps London would broaden her tastes in more ways than one.

When Jenna opened her eyes and snapped out of her reverie, she was greeted by the sight of Jacqueline, skirt hitched up, arranging her stockings, adjusting the sheer material so that the seam crawled up the back of her calf and thigh in a perfectly straight line.

'Vintage nylons,' said Jacqueline, proudly. 'Not easy to find, but I won't cut corners with my clubbing clothes.' Jenna caught a glimpse of creamy thigh at the crease where it met her ass, and as Jacqueline bent over she was treated to a flash of fully shaved pussy lips. Jenna was suddenly wide awake and horny, and had to fight the physical urge to leap up at Jacqueline, force her legs apart and suck her pussy until she tasted the juices of her orgasm. Jacqueline's voice interrupted her thoughts.

'Such a shame you can't come out. You're already famous here and no-one's even met you yet,' she said.

'How come?' replied Jenna, intrigued.

'A good dom will find that her reputation goes before her . . . right around the world,' replied Jacqueline. Jenna was fascinated by the way she could talk and apply pillarbox red lipstick to her mouth without either mumbling or smearing her makeup.

'You should be flattered.'

'Oh, I am,' said Jenna, trying to imagine those full, scarlet lips begging for mercy. And then she summoned up the courage to ask the question that was on her own lips:

'What's your thing, Jacqueline? Top or bottom?' *And man or woman?*, she also thought, but didn't say out loud. She had to know whether Jacqueline was a fuckable entity; whether to consign her adventures to fantasy or get excited that this could be something real.

'Well,' said Jacqueline, reaching for a faux-fur coat and putting her keys into her clutch bag, 'if I told you that, I'd ruin the surprise for when you do come out next week, wouldn't I? Listen, help yourself to anything you want. I'll probably stay out till at least eight, so if I don't see you beforehand, good luck with the interview tomorrow.' Jacqueline bent down and gave Jenna a good luck kiss on the forehead, leaving a waxy imprint of her lips between her eyebrows and affording Jenna a close-up view of the surprisingly round breasts which spilled over the top of Jacqueline's corset.

'Thanks, Jacqueline,' she managed to say, hoping her husky voice didn't betray what was going through her mind. 'For everything. Letting me crash here, I mean. I really appreciate it.'

Jacqueline blew a kiss in reply, closed the door behind her and was gone.

Jenna leapt to the window, and looked down at the grey shiny street until she saw Jacqueline leave through the front door and hail a cab. When she was sure the coast was clear, she began a frantic hunt for the one thing she knew would put out the fire of excitement that raged between her legs. One hand stroking her nipples through her top, the other rifled through Jacqueline's bedside drawer, blindly fumbling through a soft tangle of lacy lingerie until her fingers closed on the thing she had been looking for. As she grasped the shaft of the vibrator, wrapped in a silk scarf, she smiled to herself.

A pink Rampant Rabbit. She held it aloft like a trophy.

An expert flick of the wrist turned it on. Good: the batteries were brand new. Jenna slid out of her pyjama trousers so that she was naked from the waist down. God, she was already soaking. The tip of the dildo parted her pussy lips as smoothly as any dick could, and filled her up just as satisfyingly. Once she was happy with the weight and girth of the dildo inside her cunt, she positioned the rabbit ears either side of her clit and pressed the tiny button that set them going. At once, the intense sensations flooded her body, and the thought of Jacqueline's body underneath hers, pinning the smaller woman's wrists to the floor with her own strength . . . Jenna came in seconds. The vibe had hardly had time to warm up before she pulled it from her throbbing cunt, already over-sensitive but satisfied. She had time to wash the toy and wrap it back in the scarf that had housed it before the relief of tension triggered a fresh wave of exhaustion. Her post-orgasmic state, coupled with jet lag, sent a warm fuzzy feeling throughout her body and mind, like a glass of red wine on a winter's evening.

Jenna stayed awake for the time it took to shower, enjoying lathering herself with Jacqueline's feminine, floral products, hang up her suit for the next morning on the back of the wardrobe, and lay down on the bed to watch a bit of Sunday night TV. The next thing she knew it was 7.30 in the morning, the sun was streaming through the window onto her face, and Jacqueline stood in the doorway.

She was gloriously dishevelled, her tight pin curls beginning to drop and frizz, and her eye-makeup smudged. Red
lipstick was smeared on her neck and seemed to paint a
trail beneath her corset. Jenna wondered whose lips had
kissed her and where.

'Good morning, sleeping beauty,' said Jacqueline. 'It's
lucky I came back! I'm your human alarm clock!'

Jenna had only time to leap out of bed, shower, apply
minimal makeup, sweep her hair into a chignon and slip
into her navy Prada suit before dashing out of the door
to hail a taxi. As she left the tiny studio, she saw Jacqueline
shrug off her clothes from the night before and walk into
the bathroom. A frisson of excitement ran through Jenna
as she noticed the tell-tale red welts on Jacqueline's ass
and thighs that showed her a woman who had enjoyed a
good lashing the night before. Well, that answers my first
question – she's a bottom, thought Jenna. But is she into
boys or girls? Or, if I'm very lucky, both?

Outside the flat, Jenna switched into career mode. A cab
drew up alongside her as though he'd known she'd be
waiting for him, and Jenna hopped in gratefully. She pored
over her CV and application letter and the notes she'd
made on the department she'd applied to work for as the
cab crawled through the streets. She was so engrossed that
she didn't see the Houses of Parliament and Big Ben rising

through the sky, only noticing when the chimes sang out for 8.45 am.

To her disappointment, she didn't enter the Houses of Parliament through their imposing main entrance, but via a small annexe which was accessed by a nondescript door in a back street. She told herself that everybody had to start somewhere as she waited in a shabby ante-room with the other hopefuls. She cast a judgemental eye over them: she was confident that none of the others looked the part like she did, shabby student types who had no idea about how to present themselves. Image was everything. If the way you looked was an indicator of your level of ambition, none of these losers here could want the job more than she did. She waited for an agonising hour while the others went through and were assessed. Then it was her turn.

A secretary led her down a corridor and into the main house. Things immediately got more promising: men and women in suits strutted on red carpets down oak-panelled corridors, oozing power and influence that Jenna could almost smell. Crisp and groomed in her suit, she knew that she belonged here. If only she could talk a good interview, this job was hers.

The man behind the desk introduced himself as Simon and when they made eye contact, Jenna's heart sank. Not because she didn't think they'd get on, but because she knew they'd get on too well in different circumstances. Simon was in early middle age, a well-preserved 40-year-old, his dark brown hair thick and luxuriant, and cut into that blunt, winged hairstyle Jenna had noticed a lot of men of his class and age went for. A curtain of hair fell into his eyes whenever he looked down at his messy desk, which was frequently. Jenna wanted to push that lock of hair out of his eyes and tell him to smarten up. They stood on opposite sides of the desk for a while, a dom and her sub recognising each other by sight and smell alone. I could have you now, she thought: with the right words, I could get you hard and I could have your cock between my lips and have you begging for fucking mercy while I suck every drop of spunk out of your upper-class prick and I know it and you know it.

Damn! Jenna tried to override the throbbing that grew ever more urgent between her legs. I won't let this happen, she thought. I came here to get this job because this is what I want to do with my life, and I'm going to do it. Using all the willpower she had, and ignoring the fact that her pulse was racing, her nipples were getting harder by the second and her pussy was beginning to moisten, and certainly ignoring the fact that Simon was ineptly hiding a burgeoning erection behind that sturdy oak desk, Jenna concentrated hard and gave the interview of her lifetime.

She fired back answers to all Simon's questions with

a directness and precision that obviously impressed him, and it didn't take long for her to lose herself in the conversation. When Jenna glanced at the clock, expecting to see that ten minutes had passed, she was astonished to find that she and Simon had been talking for half an hour.

'Well, Jenna,' he said, in a tone of voice that implied he was winding things up, 'I think you've proved that you know what you're talking about, you're clearly very ambitious and intelligent, and we need more straight-talking people like you in the department.' Jenna dug her nails into her hands, willing him to hire her. 'There will of course be formalities to go through, but I'd very much like to offer you the job. It is unusual to get a decision on the spot, but there really has been no competition,' continued Simon. 'You have been far and away our best candidate. I'm sure the MP and his team will enjoy working with you very much.'

Jenna was confused for a second.

'You mean I won't be working with you?' she said.

'You'll see me around the building, but no, we won't be working directly together,' replied Simon. 'I'm chief of the selection committee for interns and researchers. I hire people, that's all.'

'We won't be working together,' Jenna repeated, as if to herself.

'No,' confirmed Simon.

'In that case,' said Jenna, 'you can take off that ridiculous suit. I'm not fucking you while you're dressed like that.'

Simon said nothing but blinked. For one awful minute, Jenna wondered if she had misread the situation. Then his lips parted and he traced his tongue slowly across his upper lip. With that one involuntary action on his part, the balance of power shifted across to the other side of the desk. Jenna finally relaxed, allowed the sensations which had been brewing inside her to spill over, to feel the twitching in her clit and acknowledge her moistening cunt.

Jenna pushed back her chair, walked over to the door and closed it behind her, locking it and showing Simon the key before placing it on top of a filing cabinet.

'Of course, I'll take off my clothes, too,' she said, undoing one button of her blouse to show she meant it, and then raising her voice to a shout. 'But only if you hurry the fuck up.'

Simon tore at his own clothes like a caveman tearing the meat from a bone, ripping his suit off, frantically. Nice tailoring, thought Jenna, watching the expensive Savile Row shirt become a worthless rag as he tore it off. His shoes were kicked off across the room, silk socks discarded, and finally his trousers he slid over his hips and unleashed a satisfyingly fat erection. Now he was naked but for his tie, which he went to unknot.

'Don't bother,' said Jenna, inspiration striking. 'We can make use of that. Now, I want you to take your cock in your hand and stroke it, making it as hard as it can be, while I take my clothes off.'

Simon nodded, a well-manicured hand cupping itself around the stalk of his prick, smoothing his own skin with fast, vigorous strokes.

'Not so fast, you greedy asshole,' said Jenna, who was now down to her bra and trousers. 'Pull your balls, slow yourself down.' Simon gave a feeble tug on the generous balls that swung low beneath his hard-on. Jenna took a step towards him. 'Like this,' she said, and yanked a lot harder. He winced, but it had done the trick. He was too turned on; he'd have come all over his own stomach before she'd even had a chance to get ready.

Jenna turned her back to Simon. 'You'd better be keeping those balls low,' she said. 'You can't come until I say so, is that understood?'

'Yes,' he gasped. 'Oh, yes.'

Footsteps echoed on the parquet floor just outside the office before being muffled by deep carpet. The thought of all the powerful people inches away from the scenario she had created made Jenna's pussy contract in a pre-orgasmic spasm.

Carefully Jenna pulled off her wide-legged trousers without removing her shoes. She hung the silk pants on the back of the chair: unlike Simon, she couldn't afford to replace quality tailoring. Yet. She turned back to face him, triumphant as his face changed and his dick twitched as he viewed her in all her naked, Amazonian glory. Her long, lean limbs and flat stomach were impressive, but it was her tits that always got them: large, round, lightly tanned, and with a swollen, rose-gold nipple perched at the centre of each firm breast.

'Kneel down,' she said, taking a step towards him. He sank to his knees immediately with unquestioning obedience. She stepped closer. 'Keep playing with your cock, but don't you dare to come,' she said. 'Really touch it, don't just pretend to stroke yourself. I'll know if you're cheating.' He nodded, helpless with lust and anticipation.

Jenna grabbed the tie that hung like a noose around Simon's neck. With one deft pull, the expensive length of silk became a leash. She pulled gently to the right, then to the left, watching as Simon's body swayed under her direction, like a horse on a bridle. She had the perfect tension: tight enough so that he had to move, not so tight that he was in any real discomfort or had trouble breathing. He was going to need all the breath he could muster for the task ahead.

Jenna parted her legs a little, feeling like the queen of the world as she towered above the powerful man twice her age, three times as rich, but utterly under her power.

'Kiss it,' she said, using her right hand to part her pussy lips so that he could see her clitoris, swollen and scarlet and waiting for his tongue. She didn't need to pull on his lead – he was in there before she had a chance to issue a further command. His nose nuzzled her clit while his tongue thrust in and out of her cunt. She could tell by the muffled murmurs he made that he couldn't get enough of the taste of her. Squatting a little, Jenna pushed down onto his face, smothering him, noticing with interest that the more she engulfed his face with her pussy, the harder he got. His absolute obedience was so sexual to her that she let rip and came, feeling the gush and laughing with delight as she ejaculated over his face. He looked up at her, his face glazed with her juice, his eyelashes bunched with it.

'OK,' said Jenna, regaining her composure even though her lips were still so swollen it was all she could do to maintain her ice-queen stance. She kept her legs apart, ostensibly so that Simon could see the trickle of leftover ejaculate as it slithered down the inside of her leg, but it was also because her orgasm had been so intense there was no way she could have closed them. 'OK,' she repeated. 'You're doing well so far. But now I'm raising the bar. Get up.' Simon leapt to his feet as eagerly as he had sunk to his knees. Jenna cast her eye around the room, looking for a suitable surface, and decided on the desk. 'Stand on the desk,' she commanded. For the first time, Simon looked uncomprehending. 'Do it!' said Jenna, flicking him in the face with the end of his tie. He did it quick enough then, wincing as his erect prick, now slick with pre-cum, hindered his ability to climb up onto the antique piece of furniture.

Standing on the desk, Simon's hips were level with her tits. Jenna took her nipple and rolled it between her thumb and forefinger, hardening the bud. She gave her own erect flesh an admiring glance before placing the tip of her nipple directly onto the sensitive tip of his penis, so that the bead of pre-cum transferred from his body to hers. She rubbed it in as though it were precious body oil. Christ, this must be torture for him. She bent down and placed the tip of her tongue against the tip of his penis, tasting a salty droplet and enjoying the tension in his face as she did so. She would let him come soon, but he didn't know that yet.

'Here's the game,' she said, lightly tugging on his balls and watching his dick bounce up an inch or two as she did so. 'I'm going to suck your cock, but you're not going to come until I give the signal. The signal will be my thumb up your ass. Don't be a pussy, you know you want it there.'

'I can't hold on,' whimpered Simon. 'If you go down on me I'll come, I won't be able to help it, you're so horny, I've never been so arous—'

'Save it,' said Jenna. 'You will be able to help it, because do you know what will happen if you come before I say so?'

He bit his lip and shook his head. Jenna took his fore-finger and bit it, hard, so that she left teethmarks around his knuckle. Simon winced.

'It's a little uncomfortable on your finger, but if I do that to your prick, you're gonna scream so loud they'll break the door down and then what will they find?'

She looked up at him, folding her arms so that her tits were pushed together. A snail-trail of his pre-ejaculate still decorated her tits. Jenna leant forward, savouring the smell of him. As well as his own personal masculine aroma, she could also smell a trace of soap. As she took his dick between her lips, she imagined him that morning in the shower, soaping his cock and balls, unaware of the adven-ture he was about to have in his own office later that day. Jenna's fellatio repertoire was extensive, ranging from the slow-burning softly-softly techniques to full-on deep throating. She judged that Simon had suffered enough and to treat him to one of her more intense blow jobs. Her mouth bore down on his hard-on as she took him as far into her mouth and down her throat as she could manage, defying her gag reflex so that the tip of his penis, the most sensitive part, was banging away at the back of her oesophagus and his balls slapped against her chin.

He was trying not to come but he couldn't help the odd thrust. She responded by sucking even harder, creating a vacuum that she knew would trip him over the edge.

He let out an animal moan that told her his climax was seconds away, and she stopped in her tracks, withdrew his penis and bared her teeth, making a little man-trap with her teeth around the base of his cock. As Jenna scraped her incisors along his tender flesh, he somehow found the strength to hold back. Good Simon. He had passed the test. She decided to put him out of his misery and into the realms of pleasure. She resumed her suck-fuck technique, enjoying the way his stocky prick filled up her face, grabbing his ass cheeks with both hands and then suddenly inserting her thumb an inch or two into his rectum. The liquid shot into her mouth in three, four, five huge pumps and the moan Simon let out was one of the sexiest sounds Jenna had ever heard. Once again, Jenna relished the power of her control: I did that, she thought, as this powerful man was reduced to the status of a help-less animal and spunk dribbled down her chin. *I made that happen.*

Easing her thumb out of Simon's ass, which elicited a fresh wail, Jenna used her athletic ability to the full, and climbed onto the desk where Simon still stood. In her heels, she was exactly the same height as him. She had one last trick up her sleeve before the adventure was finished. She pulled him close, wrapping her arms around his back and waist, some distant part of her mind realising that this was the first time their bodies had touched face-to-face like this, and leaned in for a kiss. When he realised that she was transferring all the cum from her mouth to his, he shook his head.

But his reluctance just emboldened Jenna and she took a handful of his hair and yanked and his mouth dropped open. He swallowed hesitantly at first, then enthusiastically, finally lapping up the pearly strands that adorned Jenna's face, arms and tits. She wiped his mouth with the tip of his own tie as though he were a child and elegantly slid down his body with her own mouth, easing herself off the desk, stopping to suck the last few drops of spunk from his spent and limp cock. Simon stood on the desk, dazed as though he had just been beamed down there out of the middle of nowhere. In the time it took him to come back to the real world, Jenna had dressed and smoothed her hair down, looking exactly as she had when she arrived.

'I take it I'll start tomorrow?' she said, taking the key from the filing cabinet and holding it up. Simon panicked, scrambled down and grasped for his clothes while Jenna threatened to open the door and expose his nakedness. She waited until he was back behind his desk before letting herself out. She had just one parting shot.

'When do I start?'

Simon, in his tattered shirt and spunk-stained tie, swallowed hard before replying in a guttural voice that was a shadow of the strident tones which had first attracted Jenna, 'Next Monday.'

Jenna was so elated with her new job and her new slave that she half-skipped, half-ran along the corridor. She was barely looking where she was going when she rounded a corner and bumped head-first into a man in a suit. An electric shock travelled through her as their bodies collided the same way they had at the Opera House years before: her flesh recognised him a moment before her eyes did. But it was him: that tight, square jawline, that crop of hair, those hazel eyes . . . that firm, taut chest that she had just felt, for a split second, pressed against her tits.

'It's you!' breathed Jenna, waiting for him to recognise her. She knew that in her suit and chignon she was a million miles away from the teenage rollergirl she used to be, but surely his body was responding just as hers was.

There was nobody else in the corridor. She waited, smiling, for him to acknowledge her, to give her some secret sign that he hadn't forgotten that first encounter. Her first and best slave, here, on the other side of the world. This was more than a coincidence: this was destiny.

'I'm in a hurry, you stupid bitch,' he said. 'Can't you look where you're going?' He shoved her to one side, stalking down the long corridor without a backward glance.

CHAPTER FOUR

Jenna wasted no time in establishing a base in London. Her first move was to get a place of her own to live. She couldn't crash on Jacqueline's futon forever and besides, she did not want to jeopardise her only friendship in London by letting sex get in the way – and the sight of tiny, fragile Jacqueline curled up in bed, eating toast in only her T-shirt or slipping into the shower after a night of submission was turning Jenna on so much that she knew that, if she stayed, sex, or play, would definitely be on the cards.

Jenna used the week-long window between landing the job and starting it to do four important things. Find a flat. Join a gym. Buy a bike. And find somewhere to party.

Finding a flat was easy. She simply walked into the first estate agents that she liked the look of. She told the young man behind the desk, an eager, greasy little guy with mousy-coloured hair twisted into hard little spikes, which exposed his pale scalp, that she was looking to move into somewhere within the next 24 hours. She didn't give him a chance to give her the hard sell, just told him what she wanted, the kind of apartment she was looking for, and the areas she was prepared to live in. She also made it clear that she had enough money to pay a deposit and her first month's rent in cash.

Jenna took the second flat she saw: a clean, spacious studio apartment on the top floor of a converted warehouse – modern and functional where Jacqueline's bedsit had been tumbledown and make-do. She swept an approving eye over the original wooden floorboards, the whitewashed walls, the high ceilings and the full-length windows of panelled glass which afforded a view over the rooftops, warehouses and bars of South London. Even better, the apartment was directly opposite a sleek modern gym. Across the street and a couple of storeys below her, she could see the rows of treadmills being pounded by gym-bunnies, and the chrome of the weights machines glinting in the sun. Perfect.

'I'll take it,' she told the agent, who was looking at her with an expression she recognised. Jenna knew she could have had him there and then – perhaps he was not used to dealing with women who were so brisk and businesslike. He was clearly getting off on her control and authority. But his suit was too cheap, he was too eager, it was too easy. Yesterday, she had had one of the most senior personnel officers in the House of Commons fucking her face and begging to be allowed to come, not to mention that second-chance encounter with the man from the Opera House. Jenna was on to bigger and better men now.

She took a cab back to Jacqueline's studio, where it took her five minutes to pack her case. She left a thank-you note with her mobile number by the sleeping girl's bedside, kissed her soft pale skin and inhaled her slumbery aroma. On the street, she hailed a cab and was living in her new apartment within an hour. She took off her shoes and revelled in the pure white light that bounced off the walls in this modern little sanctuary high above the city.

Before long she was over the road at the gym, paying a membership fee upfront and insisting that she got the introductory tour of the gym right now.

'You're keen, aren't you?' said the girl behind reception, eyeing the sports bag that contained Jenna's gym kit.

'I don't see the point in wasting time,' replied Jenna. 'And besides, I'm dying for a workout.'

It was company policy to assign new members a personal trainer to show them how the machines worked and devise a fitness plan. Jenna, who understood exercise equipment perfectly, as training was part of maintaining her dom's physique, was frustrated by this, preferring to be independent even when it came to exercise. But she changed her mind when she met her trainer: Barrington was a tall Jamaican with broad shoulders, huge arms, a perfectly flat stomach and an ass like two beachballs. His hair was dreadlocked and twisted into a pineapple shape on top of his head, and when he smiled a platinum-capped canine tooth flashed under the harsh strip lighting of the gym. Jenna instantly warmed to his no-nonsense, brisk style of instruction as he put her through her paces on the treadmill.

'OK, Jenna,' said Barrington, as he fitted the belt that measured her heart rate around her rib cage under her breasts. It was the first time she'd been touched so intimately for weeks, and she felt a pang of longing for another person's hands on her flesh, which she instantly managed to subdue. 'I just want to see what you can do, then we can work out a programme for you. I'd like you to run on this treadmill, exerting yourself just enough so that you're out of breath.' Jenna accepted the challenge, enjoying the old familiar sensation of running fast as her legs pumped and her feet pounded the black conveyer belt. She let the loud dance music that blared out through the speakers dictate her pace, and did not falter when Barrington turned up the speed and then the incline of the treadmill so that she was running hard, fast, and effectively uphill. It was the first serious exercise Jenna had done in over a week: it felt so good to flex her body as well as her mind. She felt the cooped-up tension of her 24-hour flight melt away.

'So, Barrington,' said Jenna, 'how long have you been at this gym?' Barrington grinned. Jenna noticed this time that his front tooth had a tiny chip which gave this big, muscular man a desperately sexy air of vulnerability.

'You're good,' he told her. 'Most people are red in the face or struggling for breath running at the pace and incline I've given you, but you're still chatting as easily as though you were strolling. You're obviously used to training hard.'

'I do everything hard,' said Jenna, looking Barrington in the eye and returning his smile. Again, she was recognising a kind of kindred spirit, but Barrington was not somebody she wanted to dominate, he was one of her kind. Tough. Disciplined. Ambitious. His reply confirmed what she had thought.

'I've only been in this line of work for a couple of years,' said Barrington. 'I was in the army for six years before that. I used to put the cadets through their paces at boot camp. And now I'm here. I tell you what, I'll look forward to training you.'

'I didn't say I was going to pay you to be my trainer,' replied Jenna indignantly.

'Yes, but you will, won't you?' said Barrington, annoyingly sure of himself.

'Let's see what you can do with me first,' said Jenna.

The next 90 minutes were an adrenalin-charged test of Jenna's physical endurance. She did 50 press-ups, 100 stomach crunches and lifted weights far heavier than any iron she'd pumped before. She came alive and responded to Barrington barking direct, army-style instructions. After an hour and a half she was shaking and had to admit she couldn't take any more. She had forgotten that the feeling you get after a really intense workout is similar to the one you get after a really intense orgasm; your mind is completely clear, your body is utterly spent and satisfied, and your limbs feel like milk and honey.

'OK, Barrington,' said Jenna. 'You're hired.' And then, as she put her damp hand in Barrington's large, warm dry one and shook it: 'You don't know where I can get a motorbike, do you?'

She signed a contract with Barrington, followed his directions to the showroom and bought herself the latest model Suzuki with the same snap-judgment determination she'd chosen her flat earlier that day. She would have loved to have bought a leather biker suit but settled for a crash helmet. She got to know the bike's weight and swing as she powered through the London streets, which were already beginning to feel like home.

The next few days were spent shopping, working out and exploring the city on foot but mostly by bike. Jenna would often cruise the streets around the Houses of Parliament and fantasise about the new life she was about to embark upon.

But by Saturday, Jenna had begun to feel odd. It was some time before she identified the vague, hollow feeling in her abdomen as loneliness. She was too proud to call Jacqueline, not wanting to appear desperate. No, she would do what she had done in Sydney and carve out her own niche. She flipped open her laptop and googled 'fetish scene'. The list of clubs that swam before her eyes was so extensive it was impossible to take it all in at once, so Jenna decided to refine her search and added the words 'dominatrix wanted'.

To her delight, the first result in her list was an invitation for dominant women to come and play that very evening. There was even a picture of the club interior: stainless steel and dark black brick gave the place a bleak, sleazy, industrial feel, but as Jenna clicked on more pictures she saw that there were also private rooms decked out in plush, dark red velvet and wrought-iron furniture, twisted metal chandeliers giving the place a gothic edge. Most thrilling of all was the picture which showed a huge cage on a raised podium in the middle of the dancefloor. Tiny thumbnail pictures showed masters and servants embroiled in power play there, faces obscured by masks or pixelated by the web designer. Jenna was pleased to note that the bodies engaged in acts of torture and sexual coupling before her were for the most part good-looking people with young, toned, lithe bodies like her own. Her eye was drawn particularly to one image of a pale, slim, naked male body lying prone on the floor of the cage, his arms and legs splayed, his erect prick deliciously vulnerable. Standing over him was a shaven-headed Asian woman, resplendent in a red PVC bra, from which hung a chain-mail skirt which only just covered her thighs and afforded a tantalising glimpse of her pussy. She wore matching scarlet boots that laced up over her knee, a spiked heel pressed into the man's chest. Jenna's pussy began to throb as she imagined herself in those clothes, standing over that man, having him gaze up at her cunt while her heel dug into his flesh, finding the soft spot between two of his ribs and pressing down just enough to make him see who was boss. Jenna's fingers travelled idly down her body, and she slid her right hand into her panties, wondering if she should get herself off. It would be so easy to gratify herself, but if she ended up going out tonight she wanted to leave some tension in her body. She sniffed her fingers before going back to the keyboard, inhaling the tangy juices which hinted at the pent-up tension she could release if she went out tonight.

She clicked back to the homepage. Her heart soared when she noticed the address; the club was based in

Westminster, not far from the office where she was to work. The place was sure to be swarming with public-school-educated, kinky, dirty British men just desperate for a taste of her own brand of Aussie-Amazonian domination. Jenna thought it would be very, very easy to make the right kind of friends here.

She showered, washed her hair, shaved her legs, underarms and all of her pussy, shivering with desire as the blade skimmed the soft folds of her cunt and revealed flesh that was tender and sensitive. Then she chose her outfit carefully. She wanted to wear something that would highlight her unique selling point: her toned athletic body, her brown sinewy limbs full of strength, rare in women on the scene. Jenna knew that she would be up against the usual pale, hourglass-figured women who could pour their generous curves into constricting corsets giving their bodies a dramatic outline that she could never hope to compete with. But few other women would possess her nut-brown skin, her muscular thighs, the washboard stomach as hard as modelling clay, the gym-honed glutes which gave her a high, round ass, the breasts which were full and firm without breaking up the beautiful streamlined sinew of her silhouette.

Jenna chose her warrior princess outfit: an attention-grabbing, traffic-stopping, made-to-measure ensemble which screamed 'I'm in charge'. It was a bra made of beaten metal, a double breastplate of dull bronze which encased her firm flesh and created a shelf for the perfect, round symmetry of her tits. No matter how hard and erect Jenna's nipples got, it wouldn't show. The bottom half of her costume was a chunky bronze belt fringed with red leather straps which covered just enough of her ass and pussy to justify the name 'skirt'. But only just. A gusset of pale red leather, like a tongue, covered her denuded cunt.

The gladiator-style leather sandals were laced up her knees, but no gladiator had ever worn shoes with platforms this high, or with heels this spiked. In this footwear, Jenna was over six feet tall, towering above the men, just the way she liked it. Copper cuffs at her wrists and around her neck completed the look. Jenna let her dark brown hair dry naturally, and it fell in wild snaky tangles around her shoulders. She wore no makeup; let the burlesque girls paint their lips red and line their eyes with kohl. She wanted her body, not her face, to stop the men in their tracks tonight. As the sky darkened, the tall windows in Jenna's apartment became a mirror, the panelled glass pixelating her reflection. She saw a fragmented image of a strong brown body which said, 'Don't fuck with me.' She threw a long black coat over her costume, and was ready to go.

Riding to the club helped to fire her up. As her

powerful motor cut through the London traffic, and she felt the wind whip her body and face, Jenna felt the familiar rush of adrenalin that always flowed through her body before she went to a new club. It was a long time since she had been somewhere entirely new where her reputation did not go before her, where she could not be sure of a friendly face or familiar fuck. The thought both frightened and invigorated her as she parked the bike in a side street a stone's throw from her office.

The interior of the club was larger and more dramatic than the pictures had made it seem, and the clientele didn't disappoint, either. Jenna nursed a Jack and coke and took in the wall-to-wall beautiful people, hungry for each other and the power play they could indulge in. She sized up a few strangers. That messy blonde woman over there, in the long white dress, looking like she'd just run away from her own wedding, was obviously out for a bit of male-dom tonight. That black guy with the black hood over his head and a body to die for was destined to be with her: Jenna knew they would end up fucking tonight and pictured their contrasting flesh, looked forward to watching them, and hoped it wouldn't take them too long to get together.

One lesbian couple were chained together at the nipples, their pierced tits bound by a long chain. Jenna watched them move, fascinated by the way their breasts pulled to one side whenever the slightest tug was exerted on the chain. A man and woman were dressed up to the nines in designer clothes as if they were going 'straight' clubbing. Jenna instantly identified them as connoisseurs of the swinging scene, out for their first taste of fetish tonight. They looked nervous but excited. If they didn't seem to have found their feet within a couple of hours, she would talk to them. She liked the idea of domming a couple, something she had never done before.

And as Jenna was people-watching, so others were looking at her. Anyone with any experience of the scene would recognise an expert dom when they saw one, and it didn't take long for the club owner to approach her. He was a tall blond man with an immaculately toned, lightly tanned and almost entirely hairless body, who introduced himself as Karl. Jenna liked his faint Scandinavian accent and the fact that he was taller than her.

'I haven't seen you before,' he said.

'I'm new in town. This is my first night out.'

'That's a charming accent you've got there,' said Karl. 'Australia, right? And a fabulous body.'

'Yes to both of those,' agreed Jenna, laughing.

'You're a top, right?'

'However did you guess?' said Jenna, flexing a formidable bicep and tapping her bronze-plated breast. They laughed again. She couldn't guess Karl's preferences, which was unusual for her. He was big and strong enough to have made a great dom, but these were often just the kind of guys who wanted to be overpowered. 'And you?' she asked.

'Depends on my mood,' said Karl.

Jenna was shocked. 'I don't believe you,' she said. 'You're either dominant or submissive: one or the other. Never both.'

Karl rolled his eyes. 'I get that a lot,' he said. 'People don't realise how fluid sexuality is. I find that different needs arise in me depending on who I'm with at the time. You, for example, Jenna . . . I take one look at you and I want to lie on the floor while you sit on my face. I want your fabulous body holding mine to ransom. But that guy over there . . .' Karl gestured towards the hooded man. 'He's one of the most brutal male doms I've ever known, he's really gifted, but all he makes me want to do is have him on his knees and fuck him in the face.'

For once, Jenna was lost for words. She believed Karl, but didn't understand where he was coming from. She could not imagine that she would ever enjoy surrendering to someone else's games. Not when the buzz she got from wielding power was so potent.

'You don't believe me, I can tell,' said Karl, smiling. He leaned one elbow on the bar, gesturing towards his glass and a barmaid with shocking pink hair and dressed only in a fishnet bikini. She refilled his glass with what looked like water. Jenna looked at the toned arm as he flexed his bicep and brought the glass up to his lips. A droplet of clear liquid ran down Karl's bare chest between his nipples, and Jenna fought the urge to tell him to lick it up. His chest really was incredible, she thought. He had an athlete's body, muscular without being bulky, and she longed to touch his skin, to find out if it really was as soft and hairless as it appeared. Usually, part of the thrill of domin-ating a man was to debase this rough, hairy creature, to know that although her flesh was more deli-cate than his, she wielded power over him. But with Karl, how would that be? To move her body against his, to lie on top of his bound body with her own smooth tits rubbing against his bare chest like two pieces of silk? She wondered if he shaved his pubic hair, or if his bush was flaxen blond like the hair on his head. She had to know. She had to have him.

She was distracted by a creak and a clank as the door to the cage in the middle of the club swung open. The hooded guy was leading the runaway bride into its centre. As Jenna had predicted, the sexual chemistry between the two was strong. She watched as he whispered something in her ear; he could see through mesh in the hood, but his lips and teeth were the only visible parts of his face. Jenna lip-read his words.

'You tempt men with your long hair and your full

breasts,' he was saying to her. 'You flaunt your young body. Are you going to let me punish you?' The woman nodded, eyes wide and those breasts heaving as her breath became shallow and urgent. Soon his mouth was on hers, probing her with a cruel tongue. They were visually stunning together, his dark skin and black clothes contrasting dramatically with her pale complexion. Her hair was such a very light shade of blonde that her white dress seemed like an extension of her flesh. Only her legs, and arms, wrapped around his body like bindweed, were distinguishable from the trunk of her body.

Karl, too, was watching with fascinated eyes, and Jenna couldn't help but wonder which position he imagined himself in: the slave, or the master? He took her hand, and whispered in her ear.

'We can watch this together from the best seat in the house.' It didn't come naturally to Jenna to let herself be taken by the hand and led across the club, not even by someone as good-looking as Karl. Normally she liked to be in charge. But these were extenuating circumstances: Karl knew his way around, and she was willing to drop her guard for a minute if it meant she got a close-up view of what promised to be some very exciting action.

Karl gestured to a spiral staircase which led to a private box with an aerial view of the cage. Jenna leaned over the edge and watched fascinated as the hooded figure began to tear the blonde's white dress away from her body in strips.

'You think that you can flaunt your breasts at me and get away with it? Do you know what needs men have?'

The blonde woman shook her head as he ripped her dress at the bodice, exposing bulbous breasts with pale pink, puffed-up nipples.

'No,' she said, in a cut-glass accent, 'no. I have never been with a man before.'

The hooded figure used a strip of the woman's dress to bind her wrists above her head and tie them to the cage. Her pale, gently curved body hung from a bar, decorated with rags of white cotton.

'Then tonight I will teach you the consequences of flaunting your body before a man.' The woman mock-struggled, but the dark swelling of her pussy lips as she flailed her legs betrayed her arousal. She was obviously no more a virgin than Jenna herself, but the fantasy was so beautifully played out that even Jenna found herself believing that she was watching someone be divested of her maidenhood in front of her. The hooded figure fumbled with his belt and unleashed a huge hard-on which was visible only for a split second before he penetrated his 'virgin' with it. Jenna watched as he speared her up to the hilt of his cock, and envied the blonde woman's rapture as he pulled at her bulging white tits with large, dark hands, letting the soft pale flesh spill between his fingers like dough, chastising her for her wanton temptation.

Jenna was now eager to play herself. She glanced down at Karl's crotch. A bulging hard-on was clearly forming within his skin-tight leather trousers. Big. Promising. There wasn't much room in those second-skin pants for it to get any bigger or harder. Surely his trapped erection would cause him great discomfort if he became any more aroused. Good. She would get him so hard that he would beg her to undo his trousers. She would get him so hard that he would think he couldn't take any more. And then she would get him a little bit harder. And after that, she would be ready to take him inside her. She turned to Karl and shoved him so that his drink spilled across her lap and stomach.

'For fuck's sake, you clumsy prick,' she scolded.

'Sorry, not sure how that happened,' said Karl. Jenna realised that the fact that she was initiating play hadn't dawned on her host. Better make it clearer. She steeled her voice.

'That was very foolish of you, Karl.' To underline the message, she slid her hand between Karl's legs and had to control herself when her fingers closed upon the full extent of his erect prick. The leather trousers constricted two firm balls topped by a rock-solid cock which radiated heat against her skin. Jenna's own leather gusset dampened as she felt her pussy lips swell and a familiar pulse begin to throb between her legs. She squeezed. Karl's blue eyes fluttered closed, and his pink lips parted. He tilted his head back slightly, revealing a prominent Adam's apple on a lean, muscular neck. His skin was flawless. No sign of stubble, not a single pore or blemish: his skin was like vellum parchment stretched tightly over a rippling body. God, he was absolutely physically perfect.

Jenna took the glass from Karl's trembling hand and took a sip. Not water after all, but a vodka and tonic. One of Jenna's favourite drinks. She savoured the bittersweet taste and gargled the liquid around in her mouth before parting her lips and allowing the sticky liquid to run down her face and between her breasts.

'Now look what you've made me do,' said Jenna. 'I think you'd better lick me clean.'

Karl slipped into slave mode as easily as Jenna was able to don the mantle of mistress. He moved with the fluid, lithe grace of a wild cat as he crouched on the seat next to Jenna. His face was between her breasts, greedily lapping up every drop of his drink from her skin. Jenna shivered as his tongue attempted to probe the skin underneath her breast armour, and felt her nipples stiffen. She had forgotten how frustrating this costume could make things; it introduced an element of torture to her own play, when all she wanted was to put her hardening nipple between his teeth and have him suck. God, she never wanted it to stop. She poured the remainder of the drink slowly, deliberately down her body, so that the liquid ran along her navel. Karl followed its raindrop trail quickly, his pink tongue lapping at her belly button.

'You've missed a bit,' said Jenna, pointing at the pool of liquid which had gathered between her breasts. Before Karl could apologise, she had pulled him by his short blond hair and forced his face into her cleavage. His legs were pressed against her knee, and she could feel his hard-on. Bigger than ever now, it must have been agony for him not to whip out his prick.

'Not good enough,' said Jenna, although it was delicious, and then, 'Lie down.'

Meekly, Karl lay on his back. Jenna crouched over him, turning to face his seat, so that her ass and pussy hovered around about his chest. She looked at her strap-laced feet over his arms, which lay down by the side of his body so that he was effectively trapped and could not use his hands to stimulate himself. No problem. Her hands would be busy enough for both of them. She tore at the leather strip that covered her pussy, found the tiny button that unleashed it and it fell away to the floor. Her cunt was now exposed to the caress of Karl's breath. The hot air he expelled between his lips fired up her pussy, made her wetter.

Jenna's hands felt for the glass tumbler: an inch or two of vodka and tonic still remained. Reaching around her body, she poured the remaining liquid between her ass and along her pussy lips, feeling the alcohol sting her skin. She felt the tip of Karl's tongue begin to lick the liquid off her asshole. As ever she loved the feeling of a tongue in her ass, the warmth and intimacy of it.

She began to massage Karl's thighs, still in skin-tight trousers, working her way in towards his cock and balls, but not giving him the gratification of laying her hands on his erection. The leather of his pants was stretched to its utmost, and Jenna knew that when she finally released that prick it would be at its peak: thick and hard and urgent and ripe. Once again, she found herself wondering whether or not he had any pubic hair, and what colour it would be. Not knowing was so delicious, imagining was so arousing, that she felt warm liquid trickle from the inside of her cunt and mix with the sticky traces of vodka. Jenna forced Karl's legs apart and placed her hand underneath his balls, directly on his perineum, the inch of skin between his balls and bum that, if touched properly, is the seat of the most bittersweet agonising pleasure a man can experience.

'Oh, please,' he whimpered, his accent stronger as his desperation grew. Jenna smiled. If she kept up this torture, she could even make him forget that he ever spoke English at all. 'Please, undo my fly, touch my cock, touch my skin.'

'I don't think I like the sound of your voice,' spat Jenna, in a cruel voice, and shifting back a couple of inches, lowered herself down on to Karl's face. A good dominatrix never shows her real feelings, and Jenna had to bite down hard on her lip to stop her own face warp from the delicious sensation of Karl's soft lips on her own cunt. Karl lapped up every trace of the drink, and when he was sucking up Jenna's own juices, the probing of his tongue became even more intense. The tip of Karl's nose teased Jenna's ass hole, and she knew that he would be inhaling the dirtiest part of her. The thought of this sent a fresh gush of juice sliding out of her pussy. She had been intending to bark orders at Karl, but he instinctively knew just where she wanted to be licked and sucked. His open mouth created light suction on the cave of her cunt, while his tongue fluttered over her throbbing clitoris.

Jenna, close to the brink of her own climax, decided that it was time to reward her humble slave. She undid the black metal buttons of Karl's fly, one by one, as much to tease herself as to tantalise Karl. The first button told Jenna that there was absolutely no hair anywhere on his body. The second button revealed the purple tip of a quivering cock, already glistening with a few drops of pre-cum. The third exposed the foreskin and the first inch or so of a beautifully smooth, almond-coloured penis. A single colourless vein ran down its length. Jenna dragged the tip of one manicured fingernail along that vein, and felt the benefit in her cunt as her flesh muffled Karl's cry of frustration and pleasure. Hot air from his mouth pleasantly warmed her underside. The fifth and sixth buttons revealed the penis in all its glory, and a pair of smooth round balls. It would have been a crime for any hair to obscure any part of this, the most beautiful penis that Jenna had ever seen.

Jenna took it in her hands and began to alternate steady strokes, starting from the bottom and massaging up the shaft of his cock to the very tip where she would twist her hand with a little flourish. The faster her hands moved, the greater the pressure of Karl's mouth, his smothered cries forcing his lips and teeth to grind against her pumping pussy.

'Don't you dare come!' barked Jenna, who was so close to orgasm herself that she wondered exactly who these instructions were for. She stopped her manipulation of Karl's genitals, made a ring of her thumb and forefinger and held it at the base of his cock. Gripping tightly, she knew there was no way he would be able to come while she was trapping the flow of blood in this way. 'Did you hear what I said?' She raised her ass off Karl's face, for the split second it took him to scream,

'Yes, mistress!' His blue eyes rolled back in his head, face glazed with her juices.

She crawled up Karl's body, lowered herself onto his cock and rode it. Its smooth passage into her cunt made her sigh with pleasure, and she decided to grant them both permission to climax.

'Now,' she whispered, and then shouted, 'Now! Fuck me! Come inside me! Now! Now! Now!' She felt the balls lift and the first thrust of his orgasm as his hot juices warmed her insides. Before he could recover, she drew her thighs up, and took herself off his cock so she was sitting on his face again and feeding him his own spunk.

'Suck it,' she commanded. Karl's tongue worked overtime, fluttering against her clit, and eventually she felt her orgasm ripple out from the hot little bud like a series of concentric circles, each one sending a stronger wave of release over her body. Exhausted, she collapsed onto her back. Karl lay beside her, and they exchanged a deep kiss, tasting each other and licking the juices off each other's faces.

'That was the best first-time domination I've ever had,' said Karl, stroking Jenna's cheek. 'You're a natural.'

'And you're a natural bottom,' replied Jenna, her tongue drawing a line from his collarbone up to his lip, which she nipped playfully between her teeth. 'You loved that so much, I just can't imagine you as a dom. I'd never let you play the top with me.'

'With you, Jenna,' said Karl, 'I would never need to.'

When they descended the spiral staircase back into the centre of the club, it was Jenna who led Karl by the hand. For the rest of the evening, drinks were on him, and he introduced her to new friends, potential partners and the club's employees, who shared gossip about the high-powered businessmen and politicians who frequented the club.

'There's usually at least one cabinet member in here on a Saturday night,' confided the pink-haired barmaid as she poured Jenna another free Jack and coke. 'You've just missed one, in fact.' Jenna wanted to ask about the man from that day outside the Opera House, the one who clearly had dealings in parliament, but how could she, without a name and only a four-year-old description of his cock to go on?

When the club closed, at 6 am, Jenna had a new playmate in Karl, and a clutch of new numbers in her phone. She thanked Karl for a great introduction to the London scene.

'It was my pleasure,' he said. 'You know that we were amazing together.' And with a giggle he knocked on her metal breastplate. 'And Christ, I'm dying to see your tits.'

Their kiss goodbye was as tender as their earlier power play had been uncompromising.

And then she was blinking in the cold dawn light,

chasing the sunrise through the streets on her bike, passing new lovers kissing in doorways, sending litter scattering in her wake. Jenna didn't bother to wear her crash helmet or her coat and enjoyed the absolute sense of freedom she felt as she crossed the river at 50 mph, breaking the speed limit, with her hair flowing out behind her and her bare skin rinsed clean by the morning air. Jenna had been in London for just under a week but already she felt that the city – and its lovers and players – were hers for the taking. She was going to find her Opera House man and make him hers. When she was on form like this, how could he resist her?

CHAPTER FIVE

The first call Jenna took in her new job was from Simon. She had barely been at her desk ten minutes, her morning cappuccino still too hot to drink, when the telephone rang.

'How are you getting on, Jenna?' he said in a voice as rich and creamy as her coffee.

'Give me a chance!' snapped Jenna. Her stern tone had the undesired effect of flipping Simon into slave mode.

'I'm sorry, please punish me,' he said, and she heard him fumble for his belt buckle.

'I haven't got time for this,' she said, and slammed the phone down. She knew that the meaner she was to Simon, the stingier with her punishments, the more influence she would ultimately have over him. She thought of him tugging his own prick in his office, fantasising about their next meeting and felt a warm flutter of arousal in her own body.

Jenna threw herself into the new job with the same enthusiasm and ambition she applied to her parallel life on the fetish scene. She soon found that her role consisted largely of menial yet demanding tasks; she spent much of her time pacing the corridors of parliament, delivering messages, carrying files, making awkward phone calls and carrying out daunting pieces of research which would have defeated a less inquisitive and resourceful mind than Jenna's. It was hard work, but she liked her colleagues, all young and ambitious and vibrant like her. Although, she often thought to herself with a smile, as they were enjoying drinks overlooking the river after work, she didn't imagine that any of them had put in quite the same kind of performance at the interview as she had done.

Jenna found that adrenaline was a funny thing; the harder she worked, the more she produced, and the only things that could bring her down and release the tension were orgasm and exercise. She was getting plenty of both, completing gruelling workouts with Barrington before work, jogging the five miles to work, barely pausing for a break all day, thriving on the busy pace, and then going clubbing once or twice a week, where she found she was making a circle of fascinating friends, Karl and Jacqueline her closest among them. Jenna had been wrong to imagine that London's fetish party people would consist solely of starchy upper-crust men in suits. In fact, her new friends were an international mix, hedonists who travelled the world looking for the next party, the most extreme sensations, and who were open to anything.

Sometimes, when it was the end of an 18-hour day, and she realised she hadn't seen the sun in nearly a week, she wondered what an Aussie-born, Bondi-raised girl like her was doing spending her life in a rabbit warren of corridors in a fusty old building in a rainy little country on the other side of the world. But deep down she knew perfectly well why she was there. Anyone who dismissed the world of politics as not sexy was seriously missing a trick. Money, class, influence, power and ruthless ambition were aphrodisiac qualities to Jenna and the air in the House was saturated with them.

And around every corner there lurked the possibility that she would see him again, feel the way only he could make her again. It could only be a matter of time. In her darker moments she wondered if she had imagined it. Not that first time in Sydney – there was no imagining that – but that second meeting, bumping into him in the corridor. Had she been mistaken? But then she thought of that chemical pull he had exerted over her and knew that she could not be mistaken. All Jenna's efforts to identify him came to nothing.

Chance, which had brought them together twice, revealed his identity to Jenna after three weeks in the job. His photograph on the front page of the internal newspaper revealed him to be Alexander Louth, MP for a run-down South London suburb but tipped for great things. Jenna let out a low whistle. His name was familiar to her: at 31, he was the youngest MP in the country and had a reputation for being devilishly clever, ruthlessly ambitious, a master of spin, independently wealthy. Jenna soon learned that his long-term ambition was to become Prime Minister, and that his reputation as a formidable politician was nothing compared to the name he'd made as a womaniser: his devastating charm and subsequent boredom and rejection had left broken hearts throughout the building.

For some reason, knowing his name and where to find him made her situation a million times more unbearable. The sexual frustration in her was like a weight. Not a metaphorical weight on her mind, but a physical load, a pain – she felt that she was carrying round a knot in her abdomen. No amount of masturbation, or exercise, or pornography, or fantasy, could displace this massive knot of tension. She would be temporarily satisfied, but within the hour she would be swollen with desire and frustration again.

There are a few ways to play this, Jenna thought. She could bide her time, continue her informal research among her colleagues and find out as much as possible about Alexander Louth before she confronted him directly.

Or – and this was much more appealing – she could continue to engineer a series of chance encounters, continue to be where she knew he would, and try to press her body against his and wait for him to yield to her. Or she could be brave and simply wander up to his office and confront him. One lunchtime, she was astonished to find her legs carrying her to the office where she knew he worked. Her tortured, longing body, it seemed, had made the decision for her. As she paced the floor outside his office, she felt her nipples stiffen and her pussy moisten. Just the knowledge that he might be on the other side of the door was enough to bring her to the brink of climax.

There was nobody in the antechamber outside the actual office. Excited as she was, the professional in Jenna couldn't help but frown at this oversight. Where was the man's staff? However, the absent desks and unmanned telephones gave her the opportunity she needed. The huge oak door which divided Alexander Louth's inner sanctum from the outer office was slightly ajar and Jenna saw that, far from being hard at work, he was leaning back in his chair with his feet on the desk, hands pressed over his eyes. His legs, encased in pinstripe-suit trousers, looked long, lean and muscular and Jenna could tell that his stomach was flat under the crisp white cotton of his shirt. A tie of eau-de-nil shot silk was loose around his neck. His hands were large, flat and masculine, the horny fingers of a manual labourer rather than the elegant, pianist's fingers that the rest of his body, his class and his accent would suggest. Just the right size for a hand to cover each of Jenna's tits, she thought, and felt the blood rush to her clit. That thought spurred her forwards, and she barged in without knocking.

'What the fuck?'

If he had been asleep, now he was definitely wide awake. Anger turned to puzzlement and then recognition and then something else – desire? Fear? Jenna couldn't tell. 'You again,' he said. 'What do you want?'

'You,' said Jenna simply. 'Don't pretend you don't recognise me. Don't pretend you don't want it.'

She could not tell if the puzzlement that creased his features was genuine or not.

'I remember bumping into you in the corridor the other day,' he said, 'and that seems to have antagonised you. I apologise but it was absolutely an accident. As for what I want, I'm not sure I understand you.' His words were politely neutral but his tone was arrogant, dismissive, and he did not bother to look Jenna in the eye as he spoke. 'If you will excuse me, I'm very busy.'

Jenna took one step closer to his desk, the block heels of her shoes percussive on the parquet wooden flooring. Now he looked up, met her eyes. She arched an eyebrow, dared him to recognise her. Slowly, deliberately, she tugged at the silk camisole underneath her suit jacket. The bra which she wore underneath was tiny, and flimsy, and easily she removed her breast, held her nipple between thumb and forefinger, squeezed it and watched it darken and harden.

'Perhaps you recognise this?' she said, and leaned forward as she tugged at her clothes to reveal the other breast. 'Or maybe this one?' Her tits were looking Alexander Louth in the eye, symmetrical and bold. 'They haven't changed much in five years, although the rest of me has. My hair is longer, and I dress in suits these days, rather than hotpants and a bikini top. Oh, and I wear shoes instead of rollerskates.' This physical description, combined with Jenna's Australian accent, was the clue Alexander Louth needed for the penny to drop. His eyes widened, his mouth dropped open and Jenna was intrigued to notice that his hand wandered south towards his lap, probably to cover the erection she knew he would be nursing as the memory flooded through him like an electric shock.

'Yeah, you remember. I made you come so hard. You begged me to touch it, didn't you? I can remember how turned on you got. And we're going to play that game again, you and I.'

But if Jenna had changed and hardened over the last five years, so had Alexander Louth. She had underestimated him. He did not rise to his feet to challenge her, but his voice was dripping with all the authority he needed.

'This is *extremely* inappropriate. If you don't leave my office this minute I will find out where you work and I will have you fired.'

This was unexpected. Jenna thought fast.

'No, you fucking won't.' Her voice was steady but her heart was hammering. 'I know you. I've had you. Have you again. And if you try to get in my way I will break you; sexually, politically, I will be the master of you.'

He stood up now, the smooth flat front of his trousers telling Jenna that he didn't have an erection. And she'd been so sure . . . Christ, this guy was a master of mind over matter. Their eyes were locked in a silent duel for a few seconds, and Jenna allowed Alexander Louth to do what no other man had been able to do; he stared her down. After what seemed like an eternity, she tucked her breasts back into her bra, and pulled her silk camisole over her naked flesh. She had come in here to humiliate, and to tease, but now she was the one who was embarrassed. The emotion was new to Jenna and she did not like it. She backed out of the room, impressed by his self-control, and completely at a loss. She had not foreseen this. His non-compliance had not been an option. She had no plan B.

Even when she was outside the door, leaving through that empty antechamber where telephones were still ringing unanswered, his composure did not break, but a hairline fracture exposed itself.

'What's your name?' he said. Jenna didn't tell him. His curiosity was a chink in his armour that gave her renewed hope.

Jenna did not know how she got through the rest of that day. She was so frustrated that she knew that even masturbation would not put her at rest. She called Barrington and asked him for a training session.

'I've had a shit day,' she said. 'I need to work out hard. I've got a lot of aggression to get rid of.' Barrington vowed to push her to extremes. Jenna rode through the London rush-hour traffic so fiercely and aggressively that she completed the half-hour journey in ten minutes.

Barrington was waiting in the foyer of the gym. One look at her face and he started laughing.

'What the hell is the matter with you, girl?' he asked. 'Whatever they done to you in that office, it can't be that bad. You work too hard. Good job you like to train hard, too. I'll see you in studio three in five minutes.'

Struggling into her Lycra workout gear, Jenna felt angry that Barrington had laughed at her, but knew that she needed his ex-army discipline to drive her to work out to make her feel better.

Barrington stood in the middle of studio three, wearing

pads on his hands and gesturing to Jenna to put on a pair of boxing gloves that lay at his feet. Double mirrors faced each other, creating endless reflections of Jenna and her trainer, making her feel dizzy.

'At times like this,' he said, 'only kick boxing will do.' He launched into the most aggressive and taxing workout Jenna had ever done in her life, challenging her to punch and kick the pads, his huge body dancing away from blows she had been sure would slam into their target, but Barrington's muscular bulk betraying the fact that he was as agile as a dancer. Frequently she would miss and punch the air, lose her balance and fall. But with every round-house kick, with every uppercut or jab, Jenna felt a little of the tension melt away. At five-minute intervals, when the sweat was pouring down between her breasts and every muscle in her body was on fire and she thought she couldn't take any more, Barrington would demand that she dropped to the floor and give him 20 push-ups. Then he would insist that she lay on her back and crunch her stomach muscles until her flesh was on fire with burning acid.

Jenna kept glancing at the clock, to see if her allocated hour was up, but the second hand seemed to be crawling around the clock face. She felt as though Barrington were mocking her, going beyond the challenge and trying to humiliate her. Perhaps she was just projecting the frustration that she had felt earlier in Alexander's office, but she realised that instead of dissipating her anger, this training session with Barrington was actually increasing it.

Time for another bout of boxing. Jenna put the large gloves on again and kicked with all her might. She found it hard to keep up with Barrington's constant movements, one moment requiring her to punch down at hip level, next thing telling her to kick higher than her own head. It was amazing that someone so large and laid-back could move so lightly. Swinging her foot too high, she knew she was going to fall. Jenna lost her balance and fell, sweaty and broken, on to crash mat on the floor. Barrington stood over her, with what Jenna felt was a mocking smile playing upon his lips. Something inside Jenna snapped and she got to her feet.

'Are you taking the piss, you son of a bitch?' she shouted, sweat from her hair flicking him in the face as she did. For once, her aggression was real and not part of some sex game. 'Because I'm not in the mood to be mocked.' The smile instantly left Barrington's face.

'And I'm not in the mood for you to talk to me like that,' he said.

'Oh, fuck you,' she said, clumsily tugging at her boxing gloves before throwing them in Barrington's face. Something in the way he calmly folded his arms flicked a switch in Jenna.

She grabbed his wrists, wrestled the pads off his hands,

and placed her hands on his forearms. She pulled the astonished man close to her, so that their hot sweaty bodies were separated only by two thin layers of high-tech sports clothing. Her breasts were pressed against his rock-hard pecs, and his soft warm prick and large balls rested just above her pubic bone. Excited now, Jenna pushed her body further in towards Barrington.

The rod below his stomach began to firm up into a hot pulsing boner. He was so big and powerful, the slightest flicker of his wrist would have sent Jenna flying. But instead she took his fleshy lips between her teeth, started to kiss him gently and then all hell broke loose. They were wrestling, with their clothes as well as each other, gasping for breath as tight Lycra was unpeeled like skin from a fruit. Jenna raised her hands over her head for Barrington to pull her body-hugging vest off her torso, to reveal breasts desperate for attention. Her Australian tan had begun to fade and her pale breasts shone like headlamps.

Simultaneously, Jenna pulled down the snug red workout pants she wore, bringing her panties with them, and kicked off her shoes. She was naked, her body glistening with sweat, her lank hair plastered to her forehead. Barrington's erection grew and strained under his Lycra shorts. He was massive.

There was no need to utter commands to Barrington: he was too near her equal to be dominated. He peeled his own clothes off without being ordered to. His cock swung upwards, reaching further than his navel. Jenna swallowed, unsure if she could accommodate such girth and length. This was a wrestling session, a battle of equals, as they grappled with each other's damp, hard bodies.

Jenna gripped his wrists again, almost ran at Barrington's body, forcing him to stagger back so that they were leaning against the mirrored wall of the studio. Their bodies were reflected all around them, an endlessly diminishing image of his strong black body wrestling with her formidable white one. Their kisses were combative, their tongues clashing and biting as Jenna climbed up Barrington's body like a mountaineer scaling a steep slope. It took all her reserves of strength to wrap her limbs around his torso and then finally lower her sodden, hungry pussy down onto his thick, long hard-on. Barrington supported her weight as the tip of his prick parted her lips. Inch by inch, Jenna relaxed onto his remarkable organ, which she felt would split her in two if she didn't take things slowly. Once he was in her all the way, she let her body go limp: Barrington made her come with several well-aimed thrusts, each one stretching the walls of her cunt to their maximum capacity. Her pussy convulsed with the strength of her orgasm, hugging and massaging his prick. It was more than he could stand, and he came then, his own legs trembling as he yielded to an intense climax.

He slid down the mirrored wall, leaving a smear of sweat in his wake, and the pair collapsed in a heap on the padded floor mat.

'I've wanted to do that ever since I first saw you,' murmured Barrington. 'You're quite a fuck.'

Jenna was reeling from the discovery that such good sex could be had without adopting her dominatrix persona. Sure, she had initiated it, and she had set the pace. But she had come, and come hard, without giving any orders or using any dirty talk.

'You're not so bad yourself,' she said, flexing her cunt to squeeze the last remaining droplets of spunk from Barrington's subsiding erection, laughing as his face distorted with something midway between pleasure and pain. 'I take it that training session was on the house?'

Jenna was not able to discuss the incident with Barrington or her feelings for Alexander Louth with her colleagues, but she could with her friends from the scene. The next day, she had lunch with Karl and Jacqueline in a café near work. Karl and Jacqueline were thrilled to meet each other, and to be surrounded by so many men in suits, and took great delight in pointing out men they'd seen at fetish nights. Jenna filed their faces away for later reference. It didn't take long for the discussion to turn, as it always seemed to these days, to Alexander and what Jenna could do about him. It became a heated debate on the nature of sexuality.

'Maybe he's just not interested,' said Jacqueline. 'Maybe he's a top, like you, and that thing in Sydney was just a one-off.'

'No,' replied Jenna. 'I know what happened in Sydney. I saw him, I recognised him. I'm never wrong.'

'People change,' argued Karl. 'Maybe he's both; maybe he just doesn't want to get involved with somebody at work. It could be any number of reasons. Why are you beating yourself up about this guy? You've only been in London a few weeks and already every sub in London wants you to dom him. You could have your pick of any guy in the city. What's so special about him?'

'Because he's a challenge,' explained Jenna. 'There's something about him I can't control, and I need to. Even if he won't admit it himself, I know that when we finally get together and he lets me take charge, everything is just going to explode. I can't concentrate on anything until it happens. It sounds stupid, but I feel that we're destined for it. Otherwise why would I have met him twice like that?' Karl looked at Jenna, his blue eyes serious and piercing.

'It sounds to me,' he said, his face deadly serious, 'that when it comes to Alexander Louth, it's yourself you can't control.'

Karl's words echoed in Jenna's head. There she was thinking that she had met her match. But what if Alexander Louth was more than a match for her? And what if that was why she was seeking him out?

Back at her desk, Jenna picked up a voicemail from Simon saying to call her urgently. Her heart sank. She was full of wine and pasta, and not in the mood to phone-dom Simon. But she called him back anyway, and was glad she had as he told her of an opportunity for promotion in another department.

'You've already outgrown the role you're doing now,' he explained. 'You will be dealing with a completely new department, and you will be heading people who have been working here longer than you have. But I think you can rise to the challenge.'

Jenna thrilled at the idea of another challenge, something to help her focus on work while she was deciding what to do about her revenge campaign on Alexander Louth.

'Sounds interesting,' she said, 'but it would have to be worth my while. In terms of money, as well as what it would do for my CV.'

'Jenna, you'd be a fool to turn this opportunity down. You don't even have to interview for it. They're desperate for someone dynamic to begin really soon, so they're taking my recommendation. You'd have a decent pay rise. Enough to buy a flat. Enough to trade your PVC whip for a diamond-encrusted cat-o'-nine-tails.' Jenna had to laugh at that.

'OK, Simon, you've persuaded me. I'll take it.' She was only half-listening as Simon described the new duties she would have and the various training courses she would need to complete to progress in her role. She twirled a finger around the phone cord and doodled on her pad; drew the profile of a man who looked like Alexander. As Simon was about to put the phone down, Jenna interrupted him.

'God, Simon, I forgot to ask which department it's in.'

'Jenna, don't you listen to anything I say?' sighed Simon, exasperated. 'You will be head of research for Alexander Louth.'

CHAPTER SIX

Jenna was looking forward to seeing Alexander's face when she reported for work on the Monday morning, but she was disappointed. His rooms were deserted. An email from Simon soon shed light on the empty offices.

'Louth is on a cultural tour of Holland. His PA and junior researchers are with him. You have ten days to get this office – which is a bloody shambles – up to scratch.

I know you won't let me down,

Simon.'

Jenna experienced a conflict of emotions. She was bitterly disappointed not to be seeing him today: she had been carrying the sexual anticipation around her like a heavy sack all weekend. But she was also pleased that she would have a chance to prove herself professionally before asserting herself sexually.

She took her first call from Alexander at 10 am.

'Alexander Louth's office,' said Jenna.

'Hello?' said a nervous female voice, obviously talking on a mobile phone with a bad signal. 'Is that the new researcher? It's Kerry here, Mr Louth's PA. I've got him on the phone for you.'

'Hello Kerry, I'm Jenna . . .' she began, but the phone was snatched away from Kerry and the next voice Jenna heard was Alexander's. His clipped, upper-class tones made Jenna wet, even though she knew he was in another country. She parted her legs and began to stroke her clit. The ruder he was, the more sensitive her clit became. The more powerful and authoritative he appeared, the more she wanted to subdue him.

'I haven't got much time, so don't bother with introductions. There's a list of letters and files that need sorting on your desk. Have them done before I'm back.'

'I'm on top of things, Mr Louth,' said Jenna, in her best phone voice which obscured all traces of her Australian accent. She tried to explain the new system she was devising for logging calls from constituents and researching possible solutions, but he cut her off.

'I fucking told you, I haven't got time for this,' he said brusquely. 'We'll meet next week. Good day.'

Jenna wasn't used to being spoken to like that, not even by people in authority. But she kept working at her clit, furiously massaging it with the back of her knuckles, closing her eyes and picturing his face, trawling her memory banks for the image of his hard dick as she came.

* * *

Jenna spent the remaining week chucking sheaves of outdated papers into the recycling bin and tidying up the office in physical as well as administrative terms. She also had her work cut out arranging a lunch meeting with the PM and his wife the following week. She was excited about setting foot in Downing Street because she knew that the concentration of power and money which went back decades would instil in her the inspiration she needed to raise her game with Alexander. She got on well with the PM's secretaries: so much more efficient than the hapless Kerry, whose lack of ambition and organisation seemed to be the main reason why Alexander's office was in such a state.

She didn't go clubbing that weekend, but took advantage of a rare and glorious sunny weekend in London, running up and down the Thames path, soaking up the sun's rays and enjoying the natural highlights and deepening tan she had by Sunday evening, when she read her book in St James's Park, feeling the chimes of Big Ben send a resonance through her primed body.

When Monday came, the heatwave showed no signs of abating, and Jenna dressed in a light linen skirt suit and a silk camisole. The look was slick and professional as long as the fitted jacket stayed on. If it came off, the silk clung to every tight contour of Jenna's athletic body. An erect nipple, say, would be distractingly visible through the sheer fabric. Jenna knew that Louth would be helpless when he saw it

He was already in when Jenna walked into the office at 8.30 am. He didn't bother looking up from his big wooden desk when she walked to his in-tray and began to lay sorted papers in front of him on the desk.

'This is your schedule for the week,' she said, pointing to the first memo. 'You and I are going to Downing Street for lunch today. This pile of papers here is department stuff. You need to sign off this bill soon. This pile of papers here is constituency stuff. I've placed both in order of what I consider to be your priorities. Oh, sorry – didn't I introduce myself? I'm Jenna Bailey. Your new head of research.'

Eye contact was made and for a few seconds there was nowhere for him to hide. He was looking vulnerable, gasping for air like a caught fish. It looked a bit like his orgasm face, she thought, remembering. Now, surely, the situation would come to a head. Now that they were working together he would admit what had happened in Sydney and they could resume the roles they were destined to fall into, mistress and slave, their night-time relationship a direct inversion of the daytime power structure. But a steel curtain of resolve seemed to fall down across his features, and when he looked at her again, she knew that he had determined not to acknowledge the past they shared.

'You seem to be on top of things,' he said, his words a sneering reminder that she was *not* on top of him. 'I'm sure you've got enough work to be getting on with for the rest of the morning. Thank you.'

Jenna stood there, arms folded, wondering how to salvage the situation. She placed her hands on her hips.

'Are you sure that's all?'

'Close the door lightly when you go,' he said, returning to his papers.

On the other side of the door, Jenna leaned on the oak panel and breathed deeply. She had expected things to go her way and she felt engulfed by a swirl of panic at the lack of control she had over Alexander. If she was honest, she was also bewildered by the lack of control she had over her own reactions. Just seeing him made her hot. How would she be able to stand working with him and not to make him bend to her will? She sat at her desk, beads of perspiration trickling down between her breasts in a tantalising caress that corresponded to the dampness between her legs.

As the morning wore on, it became apparent that Alexander's inscrutability was the least of her problems: dealing with Kerry, the PA, and Josh, the junior researcher, was going to be a nightmare. They were both clearly too terrified of Louth to defy him. Kerry was a dizzy woman in her late forties preoccupied with calories and magazines, and Josh was the kind of posh boy Jenna despised. He lacked the brash confidence she found so sexy and challenging, and was instead a wimp who spent more time on the phone asking his mother for advice than he did doing his job. Jenna was glad that she alone would be accompanying Louth to Downing Street at lunchtime.

At 12.30 precisely Alexander left his office and stalked out. He didn't summon Jenna but it was obvious that she was meant to follow him like a puppy. This she did with a sting of humiliation, trotting down the corridor after him, the heels she had worn to elongate her legs and bring a touch of dominatrix chic to her formal work clothes crippling her feet. By the time she got to the car she could feel the makeup sliding down her face – not a good look.

Once in the car, however, Jenna's mood improved. They were only travelling a few hundred yards but they did so in style, in a chauffered, air-conditioned town car which was icy cold inside. Jenna's nipples, which had remained like the rest of her body, pretty much on a state of high alert since that morning, stiffened with the temperature drop. She shrugged off the cropped linen jacket and turned her upper body towards Louth. She knew that her tits were splendid like this; the underside full and round, the upper slope smooth, the nipples slap bang in the middle. So what was his problem? The car crawled through the London traffic, sweltering tourists wandering up and down Whitehall.

To Jenna's delight, beads of sweat began to form on Alexander's lip. A corresponding slick of juice began to moisten Jenna's pussy and she extended her leg, pointing her sharp stiletto down into the leather of the passenger seat, like she wanted to do with his flesh, leaving an imprint of the pointed heel. It worked. She didn't see the bulge exactly but Louth spread out the folder that he had been reading and placed it over his lap, like a teenage boy trying to cover up an in-class hard-on with his school books. If only he would let her see that bulge, she could let the games begin.

The car swung around into Downing Street. Jenna chose that moment to pull down her silk cami and expose her left breast to Alexander while the policeman was checking the chauffeur's credentials. She spread her legs, pulled her panties aside, treating him to a view of the moist clamshell of her pussy.

But again, her tormentor proved that he was the master of mind over matter. He closed his eyes and looked away and when they pulled up outside the actual door of number ten, he had managed to subdue his hard-on. Jenna had to cover herself up with clumsy haste. Alexander got out of the opened door, leaving her humiliated. For a brief moment, she had been in control but somehow he had managed to control himself, showing that he had the greater self-discipline. And what was worse, Jenna's flashing and fantasising about Alexander's dick meant that she was now horny as hell.

Once on the other side of the famous door, she was surprised at how shabby the place was. The PM himself was surprisingly uncharismatic: Jenna felt that he lacked even one tenth of the authority and sex appeal of her own boss. More interesting was his wife, Tania De Souza, a flamboyant Portuguese lawyer who attracted more column inches than her husband for the way she combined a glittering legal career with a wardrobe to die for. Her voluptuous body, her black snaky curls and her refusal to be seen without full jewellery and makeup, even on the beach, made her a larger-than-life character. Jenna liked her; clever and powerful, witty and challenging, she felt that she had found a kindred spirit. And there was a degree of narcissism in this attraction: Jenna had to admit that Tania looked rather like an older, more sophisticated version of herself. Her body was softer and her clothes were sharper, but they were both of the same long-haired, olive-skinned type.

There was also an arrogance to Tania, evident in the domineering way she talked to her husband, that Jenna recognised. There was no doubt who controlled this relationship: in fact, Tania was better informed and more opinionated on many of the policies under discussion than her husband, and Jenna found herself wondering just who was behind many of the major decisions made about the country's future.

When all three courses of lunch had been eaten, the PM and Alexander disappeared into an office to look over some documents. Jenna found herself alone with Tania, abandoned with the PM's wife as though she were a mere consort and not his chief researcher. The slight smarted but she was determined not to show it.

Alone with Tania, there was a different kind of tension in the air. Jenna could not fully relax in Alexander's company, but felt comfortable in Tania's.

'This is your first time at number ten, isn't it?' said Tania. Jenna nodded. 'Let me show you around. We'll start with my room.'

The chamber she ushered Jenna into couldn't have been more different to the shabby, outdated décor of the rest of the apartment. This was stripped-back chic not dissimilar to Jenna's own apartment, but with the accoutrements of the rich, well travelled and well connected. Paintings and sculptures dominated the white walls. The drawn curtains were made of silver shot silk. Jenna took in a floor-to-ceiling mirror with a huge gold rococo frame, a reclining female nude painted in vivid blues and silvers, and a large chrome ornament on a plinth, which looked familiar. Jenna thought that it looked like two silver shoe-horns stuck together but that wasn't it. Tania broke the silence in her husky voice.

'So,' said Tania, 'you're working for the mysterious Alexander Louth.'

'Mysterious?' Jenna raised an eyebrow.

'He's always fascinated me. So cruel. Such a bully. Ruthless, of course, and quite brilliant. Just the kind of man who usually has a string of women falling at his feet: a wife, a mistress, a whore . . .' Jenna was aston-ished. 'He's a top, of course, but he would punish even the most compliant bottom beyond endurance.' Jenna was shocked to hear the PM's wife converse in fluent fetish speak.

'Oh, don't be surprised,' said Tania. 'I had quite a wild life in my younger days,' she said. 'You kids think you invented bondage. That's where I met my husband, in a little club just around the corner from here. Of course, we like to play in private, but I do miss the thrill of experi-menting with new lovers, too.'

Jenna's heart rate doubled and she rocked subtly back and forth on her chair, legs squeezed together, massaging a clitoris that was beginning to flicker into life for the second time that day.

'I knew as soon as you came in, Jenna. I recognise another player when I see one,' said Tania. Jenna smiled. 'You're a top, right? I bet you've got some amazing outfits.' Jenna was gratified to know that, despite her failure to dominate Alexander, her prowess was still obvious to strangers. She asked the question Tania had set up for her.

'And you,' she asked. 'What's your kink?'

Tania gave a wordless reply that was infinitely more erotic than any spoken rejoinder could have been. She stood up, undid the slim red leather belt which cinched her dress in at her tiny waist, and wrapped it twice around her neck, making an impromptu slave collar, the international and instant sign for someone who wants to be dominated.

Tania closed her eyes and tilted her head back. Her red dress hung looser about her curvy body now, but her nipples protruded and her legs were subtly parted. Everything about her was glamorous and powerful yet she closed her eyes and feigned submission. Jenna stepped closer to the other woman and with her fingers traced the belt which wrapped twice around Tania's neck, marvelling at the contrast between the shiny red leather and the soft olive flesh. Jenna pulled a little, constricting Tania, pulling the older woman's head towards her for a kiss. They paused, lips subtly touching, for what seemed like an eternity.

Then Tania slipped her tongue between Jenna's lips. This boldness could not be tolerated if Jenna was to remain in control.

'No!' Jenna pushed the other woman away. Tania bowed her head, chastened. 'My game, my rules.'

Tania nodded. She stayed still as Jenna stripped her. Her red dress hooked over her head to reveal lacy crimson panties but no bra. She looked into Jenna's eyes, her plump lips parted slightly, her pupils so dilated that her eyes were two black pools. Jenna's gaze travelled down to Tania's nipples, round and firm as Kalamata olives, on top of soft, C-cup tits. The flesh of Tania's breasts wobbled as she shook with desire and anticipation.

Tenderly, Jenna unravelled the belt from around Tania's neck. It was like a scarlet snake. Holding the buckle in her hand, she flexed it in front of Tania and watched those nipples swell a little more, lifting the breasts which rose and fell dramatically with Tania's deep and urgent breathing. With a sharp crack, Jenna brought the makeshift whip down onto the wooden floor. Tania began to moan to herself in Portuguese.

'Christ, look at you, you slut,' said Jenna, stalking around Tania's naked and trembling body. 'You can't wait for me to touch you. You like this, don't you? Anyone could find us here. If we were exposed, the scandal could bring down the government. But I can control you. You'll do anything I want you to, won't you?'

Tania nodded again, her mouth lolling open. Jenna noticed that she still wore her earrings, hugely expensive diamonds which threw sparkles of light onto terracotta skin. 'I bet you like it so much you could come right now if I flicked your clit, couldn't you?' Tania nodded again. Jenna brandished her belt again, knowing that Tania wanted nothing more than to feel the sharp smack of patent leather on her juice-slicked clit, but instead opted for a teasing tap on the underside of the woman's breast.

Tania's breast wobbled and Jenna nodded with approval as a tiny red mark appeared. She repeated the process several times, until a criss-cross of whip marks tracked the surface of Tania's breasts, like the spiky geometric petals of an exotic flower, the nipple unscathed at its centre.

'I like to see my bitches branded,' said Jenna, going over her territory and delivering a rapid but devastating series of blows onto the already tender flesh. A musky scent from between Tania's legs began to fill the room, sweeter and more seductive than any flowers could ever be.

'Brand me!' whispered Tania. 'Make your mark! Don't stop.'

'Christ, you're a slut.'

Jenna turned her attention to the back of Tania's body. The next blows she delivered to Tania's peachy ass. The swelling of Tania's behind only served to emphasise her tiny waist. She was moaning softly in Portuguese again. Jenna had to put a stop to that. While she liked to see people out of control and murmuring so much that they reverted to their mother tongues, like in a dream, Tania could have been saying anything under her breath, and that meant Jenna wasn't in control. Swiftly, she adjusted her grip on the belt so that the next slap she gave Tania's thighs landed buckle-end down. The imprint of the metal clasp on Tania's flesh was instant and gratifying. Tania began to pant like a bitch on heat.

'No!' shouted Jenna, loud enough for the policeman outside the front door to hear. 'Your dirty little mouth is allowed to speak English words only. If you're going to beg me, I want to know about it.'

'I'm sorry,' said Tania. 'I was just thinking how much I want to see you naked.'

'Stupid bitch,' said Jenna with a snarl. 'That's for me to decide. Slut.'

Pulling Tania by a coiled lock of black hair, Jenna whipped her around and marched her over to the mirror which dominated the room. Tania stared at their double reflection, the strapping young woman in the crisp suit dwarfing the elegant, dark-skinned woman who remained naked but for diamonds on her ears and wrists.

'Spread your legs,' ordered Jenna. Tania did so submissively, honey-coloured thighs parting company to reveal a dark pink pussy. The smell of Tania's arousal became stronger instantly and forced a droplet of cream from Jenna's own pussy. OK, Jenna, she told herself, stay in control. Concentrate on Tania and your own arousal will come naturally. She threaded the skinny belt between Tania's open legs, ran it back and forth along Tania's vulva. She clearly adored the slight friction of leather against the downy hair on her opening.

'Please, I'm going to come soon,' begged Tania. 'Please let me.'

Jenna knew it was time to withhold the pleasure.

'I haven't had my fun yet,' she said. What to do now? Her thoughts turned again to the silver sculpture on the plinth and a cruel smile spread across her lips as she realised what it reminded her of. Not a shoehorn at all but a double-headed dildo.

'Tania, you really are one dirty slut,' said Jenna, removing it from its plinth. It was gratifyingly heavy. 'You keep this double dildo in here waiting for someone like me to come and get your hole wet and share it with you, don't you?'

Jenna could see from the shock on Tania's face that the possibility had genuinely never occurred to her.

'It was a gift,' stammered Tania. 'From a client. It's worth a lot of money, I'm not sure we should . . .'

'I'll decide what we do with it, bitch,' snapped Jenna. 'And we're going to share it.' She placed it back on its plinth and began to undress, emotionless and businesslike, as though she were disrobing for a medical inspection. She stepped out of her shoes and panties, then took off her jacket and skirt which she folded neatly and set down on a purple chaise longue. She removed her silk vest: she wanted to feel the soft swell as their breasts met and pressed into one another.

Even barefooted, Jenna still towered over Tania. She slid one hand between Tania's legs, and inserted one, two, three, then four fingers inside the other woman's dripping pussy that seemed to have its own pulse. 'Fill me up,' begged Tania. 'I want you to fill me up.' Jenna beckoned her fingers inside Tania's cunt, felt the raised rough bean of flesh that was her G-spot, and provoked a fresh flood of moisture. Jenna removed her fingers.

'It's clear that you're wet and ready for this,' she said, picking up the silver sculpture again. 'But you haven't paid any attention to me yet. What are you going to do to get me wet?'

Like the experienced player she was, Tania dropped to her knees and, when Jenna raised one leg up onto the edge of the chaise longue, accepted the unwritten invitation to lick and suck at her clit. Jenna let herself enjoy it. No matter how much you boss a man around, only a woman can ever really know how to kiss a clit or a nipple, she thought, as Tania's pink tongue explored the bald folds and crevices of Jenna's pussy, flickering nimbly over a clit which was fast doubling in size and sensitivity, and releasing a flood of Jenna's juice onto Tania's face. When Tania came up for breath, her lipstick was smeared and her eye makeup smudged. She looked beaten, debased, just the way Jenna liked her sluts to look.

Jenna dropped to her knees so that she was facing Tania. The two women exchanged a shy, intimate smile, both knowing that the best bit was to come. Jenna placed the double-dildo sculpture on the floor between their bodies. She slid her hand between her own legs, wiping some of her plentiful pussy juice onto the smooth chrome surface, enjoying its slippery coolness. She nodded at Tania, who began to do the same. Under Jenna's command, both women raised themselves up on their thighs and hovered over the two tips of the sculpture. They both squirmed like that for a few seconds, enjoying the slippery surrender. Jenna pushed down on Tania's shoulders hard, forcing her down on the dildo so that she was penetrated before she could even realise it was going to happen. Jenna relished the sound which began as a scream of discomfort as the cold chrome entered Tania's slit, and turned to a moan of pleasure as her insides were filled and stretched to their limit.

'Can you take it, slut?' said Jenna. 'Is it too much? Is your pussy too tight?' Tania was lost in a trance of pleasure.

'Look at your reflection,' commanded Jenna, grabbing Tania's chin and forcing her head around to face the room's large, full-length mirror. When Tania opened her eyes she saw Jenna also sink down onto her end of the makeshift double-dildo , feeling every inch of her hot throbbing cunt wrap itself around this metal shape.

Both women admired their lookalike bodies which now knelt opposite each other, the silver sculpture tucked away out of sight inside their cunts. Jenna extended her legs and wrapped her ankles around the small of Tania's slender back. Their pussies rubbed together now, Tania's dark luxuriant bush rubbing furiously against Jenna's smooth mons, their clits occasionally touching, and something that felt like electricity passed between them. Their tits were clashing, slapping on each other's skin, the light coating of sweat on their bodies on this summer afternoon making tiny kissing sounds. Jenna forced Tania's head down onto her breast.

'OK, slut,' breathed Jenna, not taking her eyes off the fascinating image in the mirror, 'you can come when you feel my orgasm. I'm not far off. But if you come before me, I'll break that mirror. Do you understand?'

Tania intensified her mouthwork, sucking Jenna's tits so hard that her kisses were almost bites, to show that she understood. Jenna could now finally abandon herself to pleasure. Grinding her clit into the silky hair of Tania's mound, she pumped hard on the dildo. The massaging effect worked and she felt her cunt convulse around the smooth wet shaft. As she came, she pulled Tania's head further into her breast, until it felt like her plump lips were wrapped around her whole tit. She drew her ankles hard around Tania's waist, forcing Tania to accommodate another inch of dildo.

Jenna's climax was only just beginning to subside when they heard footsteps outside which told them the men were on their way back. Tania hadn't had her climax yet but self-preservation was more important than anything else. Pulling the sculpture out of them so fast it hurt, Jenna fumbled for Tania's dress, used it to wipe the chrome clean, and replaced it on its plinth, hastily dressing and throwing the red dress at the Prime Minister's wife. The pair were dressed in seconds. Jenna saw in the mirror that the look in her eyes was one of triumph but Tania's face registered only misery and disappointment.

Casually, Jenna forced her hand between Tania's legs and took her clit between thumb and forefinger, twisting as though fiddling with a dial on a radio, turning the tender bud almost 180 degrees. Just when she had given up hope of being allowed to come, Tania had her orgasm. Jenna felt her whole body shake against the mirror. A split second later, the PM and Alexander Louth knocked on the door and entered.

'Ah,' said the PM. 'I take it Tania's been showing you her art collection. I do hope she hasn't bored you.'

Back in the car, Jenna wondered if Alexander was tired and maybe vulnerable. Jenna, reeking of sexual satisfaction and glowing with post-orgasmic bliss, got confident.

'I fucked Tania while you were in with the PM, you know. I had her begging me to come.'

Alexander looked out of the window.

'I had a similar experience when I was 18, in Sydney, where I come from. Do you want me to tell you about it?'

They pulled up outside their office door. Jenna put her hand on the door handle and went to leave the car. Abruptly, Alexander ordered the chauffeur to continue onto his flat, informing Jenna without looking at her that he would be working from home for the rest of the afternoon.

Jenna took her soaked panties from her pocket and dropped them on the seat next to her employer. She hid in the doorway and watched as the driver did a three-point turn in the road to take Alexander away towards his flat. Briefly, thrillingly, she glimpsed him with his nose to a piece of cotton, and his hand travelling down towards his lap. The dying ember of hope in Jenna's heart flickered again and became a bright flame.

CHAPTER SEVEN

For the rest of the week, Alexander communicated with Jenna only through telephone conversations and e-mail messages, even though he was only in the next room. That thick oak door became a symbol of Jenna's frustration; she could feel his sexual energy radiating through it. She imagined him in there, secretly wanking about the things he wanted to do to her. She was sure that he was just as charged by this as she was. She had visions of using her kick-boxing skills to batter the door down and then forcing him to . . . oh, was there anything she *didn't* want to do to him? She wanted to sit on his face and smother him, tie him up, hang him up. She wanted to put a collar and lead on him and force him to eat from a bowl. She wanted to brand every inch of his skin with her riding crop, and most of all she wanted to talk him into a big fat erection which she could then wrap her cunt around. Vivid mental images stopped her concentrating at work and kept her awake at night. She was desperate for a distraction.

Fortunately, Jacqueline was able to provide one in the

form of the party of the year. She called Jenna at work, breathless with excitement because a brand new, purpose-built dungeon was opening on Saturday night, and she had VIP invitations in her hand.

'Dan – the guy who owns the dungeon – wants me to bring some players who can really put on a show for newbies to the scene,' explained Jacqueline. 'I suggested you, me and Karl. Um, I said we might be able to put on a show. What do you think?'

'Fuck, yeah,' said Jenna. She had been waiting for permission to play with Jacqueline since she had first laid eyes on her, but had not anticipated three-way action with Karl, too. Karl . . . For once, Jenna welcomed his versa-tility, his ability to switch from top to bottom at the crack of a whip. Jenna envisaged a chain of domination, in which she enslaved Karl, who in turn dominated Jacqueline.

'I'm so pleased!' squealed Jacqueline. 'And I haven't even told you the best bit yet.'

'It gets better?' asked Jenna, who was having to sit on her free hand to stop her fingers drumming on her clit.

'It does. Dan has given me a £1000 shopping budget. He says that we need to look sensational. So. What shall I buy?'

Jenna paused and considered her options.

'Do you trust me, Jacqueline?' asked Jenna.

Quick as a flash, the other girl replied, 'With my money, or my body?'

'A bit of both, actually,' laughed Jenna. 'I've got some ideas, but since I'll be playing the dominatrix on the night, I'd like it to be a surprise for you and Karl. If you hand over the cash to me, I promise I will dress us up in a way that no one will ever forget.' There was a few seconds' silence, and Jenna heard Jacqueline's breathing begin to grow deeper and raspy. She knew that she had got her way.

'I'll drop it off at your office later this afternoon.' Jenna put the phone down happy. This was one shopping trip she was really going to relish. So what if Alexander wouldn't bend to her will? The city was full of glittering, beautiful, decadent people who appreciated all she had to offer.

On Saturday morning, Jenna got up early and hit the gym for an hour or two. She wanted to make sure that she looked as good as possible this evening, and besides, a hard workout always made her feel bold and empowered. She headed straight from the gym into Soho, parking her motorbike in the midst of a group of male couriers. Dressed in her leathers, she was pleased to absorb the admiring glances from the men who hung around smoking roll-up cigarettes and drinking coffee from paper cups. Normally she would have flirted with them, but she didn't have time today. She was on a mission.

Descending the steps of her favourite sex boutique, Jenna felt her mood soar even higher. Even the smell of this place turned her on; the distinctive whiff of leather and rubber and plastic mingled with the sensual oriental oils that sizzled in a lotus-shaped burner at the entrance. Becks, the proprietor of the shop, greeted Jenna like the loyal customer she was.

'Jenna!' cried Becks. 'Good to see you. I've got some fantastic new red PVC gear in just your size.'

Jenna smiled. 'Sounds great, I'll try them on later. But first of all I've got to go shopping for a couple of friends of mine.' She outlined her requirements, estimated Jacqueline's measurements, hoping desperately that she had calculated correctly because the amazing garment that she eventually purchased would leave no room for any error.

As for Karl, he was such a regular in this shop that Becks had no problems picking out clothes for him. Jenna spent a little over the £1000 budget that Jacqueline had allotted her, but left the shop with bulging carrier bags and a sense of excitement that made her extra outlay more than worthwhile. She strapped the bags on the back of her bike and revved the engine. As she tore through the London streets, planning tonight's show, the warm seat of her motorcycle hummed with aggressive vibrations which rocked her clit and swelled her pussy.

Karl and Jacqueline turned up at Jenna's flat at five minutes past eight. They were both dressed casually in jeans and T-shirts, although Karl had brought a sports bag with him that Jenna just knew was full of his own gear – he didn't trust her. She was touched to notice that Jacqueline had brought no change of clothing, demonstrating a faith in Jenna's judgement which boded well for the rest of the evening.

Jenna answered the door in her white cotton robe. Her party clothes were firmly in place underneath and her makeup was dramatic, but she wanted to unveil herself later.

'Come in, come in, my darlings,' she said, pouring each of her guests a flute of champagne. 'I can't wait for you guys to see what I've been shopping for today. The taxi is booked for half an hour, which I think is perfect. It gives you long enough to get changed, but you're both going to look so horny that if we had any more time in my flat with you dressed in these clothes, we'd probably all fuck here and we'd never get to the club.' The others laughed, but Jenna meant it. Tonight was going to be one of her most testing exercises yet in self-control. Just the thought of Karl wearing the harness she had carefully selected for him was enough to make Jenna wet and hot between the legs; she had already soaked two pairs of panties today. And as for the outfit she had selected for Jacqueline . . . Jenna did not even dare to allow herself to visualise it, not wanting to ruin that first moment.

She drew the blinds over the huge windows of her flat, taking control, becoming the dominatrix. The blinds were white, and when they were down, the flat felt clean, bare, icy – like an operating theatre. There was something thrillingly clinical about the atmosphere now. She noticed that Jacqueline had drained her champagne flute, and that, and her characteristic blush, had flushed her doll-like cheeks. She was just as excited as Jenna was. Karl was, true to form, a little more detached, but Jenna could tell that he was only playing it cool. He just had a better poker face than Jacqueline, that was all.

Jenna handed each of her guests a stiff red carrier bag, tied with black ribbon at the top.

'Here you go,' she said. She folded her arms and watched with anticipation fluttering in her chest and between her legs as her friends saw the costumes for the very first time. Jacqueline opened the carrier bag delicately, untying the ribbon and saving it for later. Karl simply tore into his bag, throwing away layers of black tissue paper. When he saw that the bag contained only a black leather harness and a thong, he gasped with delight. He pressed his face to the soft leather pouch that was to encase his cock and balls, ran an appreciative tongue over the leather studs and buckles which would fasten his harness, looked at the long leather reins that would hook round his shoulder blades and licked his lips.

Karl and Jenna both turned their attention towards Jacqueline. With shaking hands, she withdrew her own garment, as expansive as Karl's was skimpy. Fear and arousal competed to dominate Jacqueline's face as she contemplated the super-skin-tight catsuit, made of black shiny rubber, looking too small even for her tiny body. High-heeled shoes were built into the catsuit, and a tiny black hood dangled at the neck.

'Oh, Jenna,' breathed Jacqueline, her wide eyes suggesting anxiety but the hard little nipples beginning to stiffen beneath her T-shirt and protrude through the cotton betraying her excitement, 'I've never worn anything like this before. I have never dared to. I don't know if I can . . .'

Jenna recognised Jacqueline's hesitation as a sign to slip into full-on dom mode.

'Well, it's not as if you have any choice, is it?' she said in her strictest voice, and Jacqueline's eyes began to glaze over as she understood that the game was beginning. Jenna's command continued. 'Karl, take your clothes off,' she barked. Karl began to undress, tossing his casual clothes into a pile on Jenna's floor. Once again, Jenna was struck by the Greco-Roman perfection of his body. His prick was semi-hard, and his balls, smooth and even, rose a little as he tried to contain his excitement. Jenna manhandled him into the harness. Two bolted leather straps like skinny belts ran above and below his nipples, and more encircled his upper arms. Jenna fastened the harness at the back with the buckle. 'Is that too tight?' she asked Karl as she drew the leather tight against his body, squeezing out his perfect flesh. He winked and nodded. Mercilessly, Jenna drew the band even tighter. The leather would rub and chafe at Karl's soft skin and by the end of the night this slave would be branded. She pulled the long leather straps that dangled from his shoulder blades and watched with satisfaction as his upper body jerked back. Karl's feet were hip-width apart as Jenna slid the thong through his parted thighs and fastened the jockstrap just a little tighter than was comfortable again. It cut underneath his buttocks, but left his asshole open for play. Karl's erection was trapped in soft black rubber and leather. Just the way Jenna wanted it.

Meanwhile, Jacqueline was holding the black latex up to her skin, feeling its sticky, tacky surface against her peachy soft cheek. Her nipples were now like little pegs sticking through her top, and Jenna was sure she could smell the other girl's arousal. 'OK, Karl, it's going to take two of us to get this little slut into her new costume.' At the words 'little slut', Jacqueline's lips parted and her heavy breathing became shorter and more desperate. 'I'll hold her down while you get her naked.' Karl, clearly loving this combination of being ordered about by Jenna and dominating Jacqueline, obeyed with delight. Jenna held Jacqueline's slim wrists, splaying her arms, while Karl mercilessly tore away at her clothes, pulling jeans down over skinny hips in one swift movement. Jenna gasped as she saw Jacqueline's bush, a neatly trimmed flash of flame-orange hair which seemed to glow between her legs. She gripped Jacqueline by the hips and ran her fingers through her downy pubic hair while Karl yanked her T-shirt over her head.

'Christ, she's soaking,' Jenna remarked, rapidly sliding a finger into Jacqueline's dripping hole and feeling its wet walls convulse around the digit. Her own pussy pulsed in response. 'The dirty, dirty little slut.'

Karl covered Jacqueline in baby talc to ease her into the skin-tight catsuit. Dusted with white powder, she looked more fragile and vulnerable than ever.

Jenna laid the catsuit out on the ground, spreading it out into a star shape. Zips and buckles broke up the expanse of black latex, and Jenna watched as the other two realised exactly what those zips and buckles were for. The room was charged with arousal and anticipation.

'Stand here, slut,' ordered Jenna, pointing to the spot directly in front of the catsuit. Obediently, Jacqueline padded across the room, leaving white baby-powder footprints in her wake. Karl, obeying the wordless command of Jenna's stern glance, forced each of Jacqueline's feet into the cruelly high-heeled shoes, half a size too small for even Jacqueline's dainty toes. It took both of them to stuff her flesh into the tight, unforgiving black latex, rolling it first up her legs, then over her hips and ass. As her white flesh was swallowed up by a black second skin, Jacqueline closed her eyes and sighed, her small breasts rising and falling rapidly as her breathing became shallow. Soon those tits were flattened, forced into the catsuit, her hands were eased into rubber gloves and the only part of her body uncovered was her face. Pale and beautiful, with a tumble of red-gold curls surrounding her head like a halo, Jacqueline looked like some kind of fallen angel. Jenna allowed the zipped hood to hang loose around her slave's neck. For now.

Karl too looked like a perverted cherub in his black leather harness and jockstrap. Jenna thought the time was right to slip out of her white robe and reveal the red one-piece she wore. It was intricately made in leather and chainmail, so that at first glance it looked like a spider had spun a web on her body in blood. The slaves gasped.

'Don't speak,' ordered Jenna as she laced her favourite platform-soled boots up to just over her knee. 'Jacqueline, you are not to speak without my or Karl's permission all night. I don't care how horny you get, or how near to coming, you keep your pretty little mouth closed and if you meet this challenge then I will permit you to climax. Do you understand?' Jacqueline nodded. Jenna turned to Karl.

'Karl, you're only allowed to speak to Jacqueline. You may not directly address me. Understood?' Karl's hard-on, straining in his trousers, confirmed his acquiescence. As they left the apartment, Jenna remembered the final, most important thing about the game they were about to play. 'Our safe word tonight is "Red Cross". If I go too far, or if you get frightened – bad frightened, not good frightened – just say "Red Cross" and I will let you go.'

Luckily Jenna had pre-booked a taxi, and she allowed Karl and Jacqueline to wear coats to the club. It was somewhere in yet-to-be-redeveloped outer London, on what looked like a run-down industrial estate. As the taxi weaved its way through seemingly abandoned building sites, wire-mesh fences dividing the deserted road from abandoned warehouses and crates and scrapheaps, even Jenna began to feel nervous. It was hard to believe they were in London; it was more like being in the war zone of a foreign country. More than once, the driver stopped to consult his A–Z, muttering that in 20 years of working in the capital he had never once come across this area or one like it.

Jenna disliked the way he questioned her authority: it undermined her in front of the two slaves who sat mute in the back seat. But her doubts were quickly and suddenly assuaged when the taxi driver took a sharp left and plunged into an empty street where there was a single, anonymous-looking building. A door in the wall was discreetly marked with a red cross. Jenna paid off the driver, tipped him, and she and her slaves were alone in the night. Someone must have been watching because even before Jenna could bring a raised fist down on the door to knock, it swung open, and they were led down a long, dark corridor, lit only with flaming torches held by wrought-iron candelabras. The walk down to the crimson velvet curtain at the end of the corridor seemed endless, and once they had showed the clipboard girl their invitations, the three passed through that heavy drape and entered another world.

Vast as a tennis court, the room was decorated in black and steel, giving the place an edgy, industrial feel. Glass windows surrounded empty beds, so that the people who were playing behind them would feel watched as though in a fish tank. Private bunks, like catacombs, were dug into the walls and illuminated by spotlights; Jenna looked forward to watching people fucking heavily in those cubby-holes before the night was through.

The centre of the room was dominated by a circular bar. Nothing unusual about that, but the Perspex bar was half filled with water and a man and a woman in bondage gear floated in the narrow, constrictive pool, lit up by underwater spotlights. This place had clearly been custom-designed with pleasure and torture in mind.

A stocky, Italian-looking guy bound over to Jacqueline and kissed her on both cheeks.

'Jackie, darling,' he said in a low, mellifluous voice. 'So glad you came. Now you and your friends are here, the party can really get started. What do you think?' Jacqueline fixed silent round eyes on Dan's face.

'You may speak,' Jenna said. But Jacqueline didn't get the chance.

'Ah,' said Dan, understanding at once. 'Your game has already begun. I will address the woman who is clearly mistress of this group.' He turned to Jenna. 'And you must be Jenna. Your reputation goes before you.'

'Glad to hear it,' she said. 'And this is Karl. He is second in command, but the pair of them will only be allowed to communicate through me.'

'Let me get you all a drink,' Dan said, gesturing to one of the bar staff who immediately proceeded to mix elaborate cocktails for them. As they sipped, Dan told them that he wanted the real show to start at about 11 o'clock. Jenna looked at the old-fashioned grandfather clock on the wall, which had a single handcuff swinging in its casing instead of a pendulum. Twenty minutes to go. She decided to warm her slaves up a little bit. A sharp tug on Karl's reins made him jerk and spill his drink down his chest.

'Lick that up, slut,' said Jenna to Jacqueline, without looking at her. Jacqueline fell upon Karl's smooth chest, greedily devouring the droplets of liquid. When she had finished, Jacqueline sat back.

Jenna carefully, slowly unfastened the two zips on Jacqueline's breasts, so that her flesh squeezed through the opening as though gasping for air. The exposed tits were compressed and firmer than ever. Jenna ordered Karl to whip her lightly with his fingertips. He did so, flicking the flesh, which wobbled like a tiny jelly. Jacqueline looked like she would die from pleasure. The nipple darkened and swelled.

'Your breasts betray the fact that your punishment excites you, slut,' said Jenna. 'Let's see if the rest of your body is so easy to turn on.' With strong, rippling arms, Karl forced Jacqueline's knees apart. Quick as a flash, Jenna was in there, unzipping the shiny black fastening that covered Jacqueline's pussy. The flesh beneath was pink and dripping. Clear liquid oozed from inside the latex and ran down Jacqueline's inner thigh. Jenna gestured towards the juice. Karl bent double and began to lap it up like a cat drinking milk from a saucer.

'Don't you dare lick her cunt,' dictated Jenna. She didn't want them both getting too horny too soon. Looking around with frustration, her eyes alighted on the glass screen which divided the central playroom from the rest of the club. 'Come with me.'

Jenna paused, looked Jacqueline up and down and made eye contact with the girl to check she was really fine with this. Jacqueline's dilated pupils and flushed cheeks and wide smile reassured Jenna that she was more than OK, she was in her own special kind of heaven. In fact, thought Jenna, Jacqueline looked ready for her to turn the pleasure/pain up a notch or two.

While Karl watched, Jenna drew Jacqueline in towards her. Wrapping strong muscular arms around the smaller, slighter girl's body, Jenna felt empowered by her physical strength and superiority. Jacqueline's puffy nipples poked through the slits in her suit and gently prodded at Jenna's own body, growing hard as they brushed against the filigree of her dress. Jenna imagined Jacqueline's tits as tiny insects getting caught in a spider's web. The thought made her warm and wet between her legs. She felt the fluid begin to pool in the gusset of her red panties and pressed her lips on Jacqueline's, forcing her tongue into the other girl's mouth, not that she met with much resistance. Then, before anybody knew what she was doing, she pulled that black plastic hood up and over Jacqueline's head, the noise of the zip clearly audible as she secured the seal down the centre of Jacqueline's face, obscuring the girl's eyes, blocking her nostrils, and leaving only the mouth visible, turning her from fallen angel to helpless gimp in two seconds. Karl's hands wandered to his cock, but he dared not release his erection from its tight pouch without permission from his mistress.

Jenna hooked the reins over Karl's shoulders so that she was leading him like a camel through the desert. He in turn led Jacqueline by the hand into the glass play-room. The club was filling up now, and a crowd of people gathered around them, but the steward on the door shook his head, emphasising that only three people were to be allowed at this time.

Slapping Karl's hand away from the gimp, Jenna wasted no time in throwing Jacqueline face down on the bed. Jacqueline's exposed, bulging pussy was wetter and pinker than ever, and the smell of her arousal and of Jenna's own musk and of Karl's fresh sweat filled the tiny room, infusing it with the unmistakable, irresistible aroma of desire.

'Right, this is how it's going to be. Jacqueline, you're going to spread your eager little pussy and someone is going to fuck you. From behind. It might be Karl's cock, it might be my hand, it might be Karl's hand and maybe, if you don't disguise your pleasure, you'll find that my crop comes raining down on your dirty little cunt.' At these threats Jacqueline's pussy began to twitch convulsively.

Jenna led Karl over to the prone Jacqueline. She had never seen him in dom mode before, and had to admit that the cruel twist on his lip suited him.

'Talk to her,' said Jenna. Karl knelt between Jacqueline's

legs and blew on her moist pussy. Steam rose from between her legs as her body heat evaporated into the cool, air-conditioned club.

'So hot, and so wet, you dirty little bitch,' Karl murmured. Jacqueline could obviously hear through her mask, as she nodded her head in agreement. Jenna heard squashed tits making squeaking noises against the latex mattress and grew wetter.

'Get inside her,' commanded Jenna, too quietly for Jacqueline to hear, and undid the buckle that fastened Karl's pouch. The soft leather cup fell away, leaving his hips and butt bound with leather straps, but his prick bouncing and unleashed, the hardest, thickest erection Jenna had seen in a long time.

Karl was inside Jacqueline in seconds, the two bodies bucking and rising in a perfect, mutually understood motion. Karl's pale, solid, muscled body dwarfed Jacqueline's tiny black frame and as they stifled their cries for fear of punishment, Jenna thought it was almost a shame to join in such a perfect union. But Karl was having too much fun and if she did not assert her authority soon, he would slip out of her control.

She turned her attention away from her slaves for a second, and looked at the glass-panelled walls which enclosed them. The sight was disarming. Bodies pressed against the glass, on all four sides, breasts and cocks and mouths and arms and hands jammed up against the glass, sweat and steam from people's breath and body oils smearing the glass and sending the writhing bodies into soft focus. Some of them were touching each other, some of them touching themselves, and even as Jenna looked, the crowd became two, then three people deep. It was like having four television screens surrounding her, each one playing a different pornographic film of a group sex scene. But what she noticed most was the eyes; all of them trained on her, waiting to see what this mistress who had these two bodies utterly at her command would do next.

Well, she couldn't let them down, could she? From her bag, Jenna produced a red strap-on harness which she proceeded to fasten around her hips. The scarlet, nine-inch dildo protruded from her mons pubis. A tiny, carefully positioned nub of plastic at the base of the dildo also massaged her clitoris through her panties. She would appreciate that when she started thrusting. A murmur of arousal, like a Mexican wave, went through the watching crowd. Karl, innocent of the surprise coming his way, was lost in Jacqueline, his arms pinning hers to the bed, his eyes closed with pleasure and the effort of trying not to come.

Jenna took a generous-sized dollop of lube from the dispenser on the wall and smeared the cold liquid around Karl's smooth, hairless, twitching sphincter. The tight muscles of his perfect ass contracted and relaxed in anticipation. He was probably only expecting a finger or thumb, and didn't know what was coming to him. Jenna changed that by pressing the cold plastic dildo tip between his cheeks, exploring the highly sensitive entrance to his ass hole. Then, with the merciless treatment that slaves deserved, she pushed her hips forward so that Karl's tight little opening was crudely penetrated.

The thought of Jacqueline on the bottom of this three-person pile-up, crushed by the weight of Karl's body which was in turn weighed down by Jenna's thrusts, caused Jenna's nipples to harden: one rogue nipple escaped from her dress and stuck out between two red chains. She used the reins to pull Karl's upper body back, so that his hips were stuck in between hers and Jacqueline's. With every thrust, Jenna felt her own pussy grow hot and wet, and the drumming in her clit grew more rapid and urgent. The tiny nub of plastic, carefully designed to stimulate either side of her clitoris but teasingly not touch the bud itself, was doing its job.

Underneath her ministrations, she could tell that both Jacqueline and Karl were desperate to come. Karl's body was subject to a series of violent convulsions, while Jacqueline's rubber-clad arms and legs were flailing and clutching at thin air as her whole body tried to resist the inevitable climax. Jenna looked at her audience, a sea of writing bodies pressed against the glass, and arched an eyebrow. As one, they understood her unspoken question: should she show mercy to her slaves and let them come? Their contorted faces told her that they too were desperate for the release that only she, Jenna, could give them. She felt like a goddess, holding in her hands the power to unleash something that gave a complete new meaning to the word multiple orgasm. Throwing back her head, so that her dark snaky curls tumbled down her back, and raising her arms so that her splendid round breasts were clearly visible through the lines of her dress, she uttered a single word.

'Come!' she commanded, and they did. All of them. Not just Jacqueline and Karl, whose convulsions and juices she could feel and smell as they surrendered to the most intense orgasms they had ever had, but also the sea of bodies around her tensed and relaxed as their own orgasms engulfed them. Eyes were closed, lips were parted, strangers clutched at each other's mouths and breasts, wanting to connect with as much flesh as possible to intensify this shared orgasm. Jenna felt as though she were the conductor of a mighty orchestra of human bodies and that this was the crescendo, the highlight of her symphony. It should have been the biggest power trip of her life.

But then she saw him: unmoved and unmoving in the midst of a sea of orgiastic bodies. He was wearing a tight black T-shirt that showed off his broad, muscular chest, and an iron mask in a vain attempt to disguise his identity, but Jenna would have recognised the set of that jaw and that rich, caramel-coloured hair anywhere. Alexander Louth folded his arms and remained impassive while all those around him were overwhelmed with sexual pleasure. Jenna's own orgasm, which had been building at the tip of her clitoris, suddenly subsided and vanished as though it had never been there. Every fibre of her being wanted to call his name, to pull her dildo out of Karl's bulging, meaty ass hole, to abandon her two favourite slaves, but the one thing a dominatrix can never do is lose her cool. And the one person Jenna did not want to lose her cool in front of was Alexander. She called the shots in these games; there was no way she was going to let him humiliate her. In the time it took for her to even have these thoughts and blink, he was gone again.

Jenna unstrapped her harness from her thighs and left the shaft still sticking in Karl's arse. It would not do him any harm to be humiliated while it remained there for a couple of minutes. Knocking on the glass, she selected a slack-jawed young man whose build and face reminded her vaguely of Alexander and beckoned him into her mistress's chamber. Pulling her leather panties to one side, Jenna ordered him to lick her until she came. Briefly he dropped to his knees, hypnotised by Jenna's clit, his gaze occasionally darting towards the other side of the bed where Karl still lay on top of Jacqueline in her gimp costume, a big red dildo sticking out of his behind. The stranger was an obedient slave, and as his tongue flickered deftly and eagerly over her clit and probed the outer edges of her cunt, Jenna felt that fugitive orgasm return to her, as the tension began to build in her thighs and pelvis.

'Suck it, slave,' she said in her best dominatrix voice. The man between her legs obeyed, creating a tiny vacuum on her clit which finally brought forth the hot, wet, preclimactic flutterings that told her orgasm was now inevitable. But instead of opening her eyes and gazing at the sea of adoring faces on the other side of the glass, Jenna found that all she wanted to do as her orgasm washed over her was to close her eyes and pretend that the lookalike between her legs was really Alexander Louth, debased, obedient, the arrogant and powerful man transformed into Jenna's willing slave.

CHAPTER EIGHT

Jenna felt nervous when she entered the office on Monday morning. She was sure Alexander had been in the club, and just a couple of weeks ago, she would have come right out and asked him what the hell he thought he was playing at. But she didn't feel able to. Alexander was doing something to her, robbing her of the one thing she'd always been sure of: her ability to kick ass in any situation. As the day wore on and his face remained as inscrutable as ever, her resolve not to mention the incident strengthened. She didn't want to give him the satisfaction. If he wasn't going to play by her rules, she sure as hell wasn't going to play by his.

Instead, she was super polite and deferential. She didn't quite stoop to Kerry and Josh's level of timidity, but she ceased all her suggestive behaviour and poured all her energies into working for Alexander. The harder she worked and the better results she got, the more dismissive and rude he was. The more he distanced himself from her, the more she wanted him, so the harder she worked to distract herself and prove herself. It was a vicious circle.

She soon found herself working late with him three or four nights a week. It nearly killed her to be so close and not barge into the office, straddle him and order him to fuck her, but she held her ground. Thank God for Barrington, Karl and Jacqueline, all ready and willing for her to take out her frustrations on them at the end of another long working week. They had grown tired of her talking about Alexander, but Jacqueline and Karl never tired of her binding and blindfolding them as she tongue-bathed their flesh, brought down a lash, teased them to the point of orgasm, walked on them in high heels, and Barrington was always at the ready when she suggested a horizontal workout. She was even resorting to domming Simon again: whenever Alexander really pissed her off she'd call Simon and demand that he be naked and hard in his office (and then not turn up for an hour). And then there were the procession of faceless slaves in clubs . . . Jenna wondered just how many bodies and minds she would have to master to satisfy the lust Alexander had awoken in her.

The side effect of Jenna's hard work was that the department and Alexander's career continued to rise and rise. Her reputation as a spin doctor and speech writer was growing, and Simon assured her it was only a matter of time before she was poached by an even more successful MP – a member of the Cabinet, perhaps. She wasn't sure how she felt about that.

Work, home, gym and clubbing blended into one another as Jenna continued to play as hard as she worked. The surface of her desk was tidy but the space underneath it was out of control. Books, CDs, magazines, crash helmets and motorbike leathers, gym kit and shopping piled up under her desk. There was a pair of crystal-encrusted handcuffs she was saving for Karl and a strappy peephole leather garment she had bought for Jacqueline. It was made of thin red and black leather straps and looked rather like a swimming costume, if a swimming costume bit into the flesh and exposed the breasts, back, belly, ass and pussy, that was. In times of stress, Jenna would open the bag and caress it, promising herself that when she finally forced Jacqueline into it, all her tension would melt away.

Until the day she looked underneath her desk and the bag had gone. Jenna's blood ran cold. Surely the cleaners wouldn't have it, and Kerry or Josh would never go under her desk. There was only one other person with access to it: Alexander. She rummaged frantically under the desk, looking for it, and a shiver on the back of her neck told her that he was watching her. She looked up.

'Looking for this?' he said, his full lip curling into a sneer. Jenna was surprised and ashamed to find that she was shaking. 'I could sack you. What if a visitor found this? Having this kind of crap in my office is just asking for a scandal. This is going to go on your employment record.' He walked over to a filing cabinet and pulled out a foolscap file in a dull emerald green. 'I had given you an exemplary record despite your attempts at harassing me because you're good at your job. But I'm going to change that now, and make you deliver the file to HR yourself.' He opened the file and began to write in it.

Jenna smirked: that would go through Simon and she'd be able to cancel it totally. Alexander saw the fleeting smug smile and a shadow fell over his face, his features inscrutable and his eyes glinting like steel.

'Or I could punish you myself, here and now.' At the word punish, usually her command, Jenna felt her stomach flip and her pussy contract. A hot, wet flood moistened her panties. This was the wrong way around, surely?

'It's dress-down Friday, after all,' he said. 'Why don't you slip into something more uncomfortable?'

Jenna didn't know what she was doing as she removed her wrap dress, then her bra and her panties. Alexander held out the playsuit which had been custom-made for dainty little Jacqueline, and as if on auto-pilot, Jenna climbed into it. She had never felt so close to orgasm in her whole life: her entire body seemed to be plugged into an electric circuit, her skin alive to every light touch as she let Alexander force her arms and legs into the garment. Even on its loosest notch, it was far too tight for Jenna's strapping frame. The belt between her legs dug in even tighter than it was supposed to, the thin leather strip dividing her body, resting directly on her clit and squeezing her pussy lips out the sides. He did the buckle up with a little yank.

'Oh dear,' he said, in mock disappointment. 'This doesn't seem to be quite your size.' The shoulder straps dug into her flesh like a too-tight bra and the toned, firm flesh of her back spilled over the back strap. The straps were just right to encircle Jacqueline's petite bosom, but stuffing Jenna's full and bulbous breasts in them was another matter entirely. Alexander pulled mercilessly at her breasts, forcing the excess flesh through the tiny opening, so that her tits spilled and poked out. The roundess of her nipples was grossly exaggerated and Jenna found them super-sensitive. They swelled fast, hard nipples pointing towards Alexander, as though they were begging for his attention and his touch. His hands were all over her and as she felt her skin come to life she realised that that was all that really mattered.

Alexander stood before her, folded his arms, reached out and gave each constricted breast a tiny slap.

'Dear me,' he said. 'That really is a terribly restrictive garment. I don't know how you're going to deliver your file wearing that. It's a long walk through the corridors.'

She held out her hands for the file but Alexander had

clearly been through the clutter under her desk more
thoroughly than she had first thought. He produced the
glittering handcuffs Jenna had intended for Karl. She felt
her pussy throb with the nearness of his body and the
masterful touch of him as he laced her hands behind her
back and snapped shut the cuffs. With her shoulders pulled
back, her tits felt more exposed than they ever had before.
Her darkening erect nipples, like two pegs, told the story
of her growing arousal. She opened her mouth to speak
and Alexander put the file in her mouth. With a sinking
heart she realised that she would have to take it to Simon.
For anyone to see her like this would be awful, but for it
to be Simon, the man who so respected her as a dominatrix, it would be unthinkable.

'Down the corridor,' he said. 'You know where it is.
I doubt he'll be there, but I'll enjoy watching you leave
it under his door if not.'

She poked a nervous head out of the door, and stepped
into the seemingly endless passageway. A stubborn voice
inside Jenna's head said, You're not going to treat me like
that, this is my job. Her body's reaction told a different
story. Her feet were carrying her in the direction of Simon's
office, a five-minute walk. Already the gusset of the harness
was damp with her juices, and the musky smell of her
arousal mingled with her perfume and the fusty odour of
the old corridors and the floor polish the night cleaners

had recently applied. She could hear their machines a few floors away. The knowledge that they could see her at any moment only served to intensify her arousal. She was on the receiving end of the kind of punishment she usually dished out, and she loved it. Her bare feet made tiny slapping sounds on the wooden floors and were silent on the carpeted areas. Behind her, Alexander's expensive leather-soled shoes made almost no sound, but his heavy breathing told her that he was following her, watching to make sure she did not cheat.

Draughts whistled up and down the deserted corridors, making her skin turn to gooseflesh, which only made her tits poke out even more. The only heat in her body seemed to be a warm moisture between her legs, which she could not stop. In fact, it got worse with every step she took. The thin leather strap between her legs stimulated her clit with every move. She spread her legs a little, walking like a rider without a horse, to ease the tension and try to keep her climax under control.

'Jenna, don't walk like that. I want to see you sashay like Marilyn Monroe, one leg in front of the other.' She obeyed, and found her clit begging for mercy, for release. Every step she took, every corridor and blind corner presented the possibility that she would walk into someone she knew. It didn't take a genius to work out that parading through the House of Commons, late at night, naked but for a too-tight body harness counted as gross misconduct and was a sackable offence. I can stop this whenever I want, Jenna told herself, but she knew it wasn't true. Step by agonising, delicious step, she made her way to Simon's office.

The door, thank fuck, was locked. At least Simon wouldn't be there to see her humiliation. Jenna opened her mouth and dropped the file on the floor. There was a tiny gap beneath the floor and the door, and Jenna made to kick the paper through with her toe.

'Stop,' said Alexander, and his voice was terrifyingly powerful. 'Using your feet is cheating. Bend down and push it through.'

Jenna, hands shackled behind her back, knew that he meant her to do it with her mouth. She just maintained her balance as her muscular thighs flexed and then dropped to her knees with the control and grace of a ballerina. The leather straps cut into the top of her ass crack and dug into her shoulders like a blade, but she didn't wince. She was distracted by the way it pinched her clitoris, sawing away at the tender bud and half-numbing it. The lower strap pushed on her bladder, causing her discomfort. Her nipples brushed the floor as she used her nose to shove the file, inch by inch, underneath the door. A tiny wind whipped through the gap and blew dust into her face and eyes and mouth.

She blinked away the spontaneous, protective tears that her eyes formed and spat out the dust.

She had completed her task. She looked up at Alexander expectantly, wondering what was next. Christ, he looked horny: not a hair out of place, even his gold tie-pin totally straight, his collar and cuffs as clean, his suit perfectly pressed. Only the rod of flesh encased in his crotch and a throbbing vein on his temple gave any indication that he was aroused. Jenna was struck by a vision of herself fucking Alexander but instead of the usual mental images of riding him like a pony, of being on top and in control, in this fantasy she was crushed beneath his masculine bulk, lying on her back, motionless and feminine and vulnerable while his cock found her cunt and sliced into it like a hot knife through butter. The power of this image was so surprisingly strong that Jenna felt herself let out a wail of frustration and longing.

'Shhh,' said Alexander. 'Someone might hear you, and we can't have that, can we? I think we should get you back to my office where we can't be heard.' Jenna rose to her feet with an athlete's control and strength in a single bound, only to find Alexander was shaking his head. 'I don't think standing up will be necessary,' he said. Next thing Jenna knew, he had hold of her wrists, and yanked them painfully over her head so that she lost her balance. She fell backwards, but instead of catching her, he let her fall, pulling on her hair so that he was dragging her by the hair and wrists. Jenna felt her legs and thighs graze against polished floor and burn on carpet as he pulled her along like a caveman dragging his woman back to his lair. Occasionally, he would hook a finger underneath the shoulder strap of her harness, pulling it tighter over her. She closed her eyes, not because she didn't want anyone to see her any more but because the mere sight of her constricted breasts made her want to come, and she wouldn't let her satisfaction be his.

Jenna knew she was back in his office when the door slammed and he bolted it and let go of her wrists and hair. She opened her eyes and lay panting on the floor, letting the feeling come back to her wrists and her tingling clit. He stood above her, still fully dressed.

'You didn't think it would end up like this, did you?' he breathed, smacking her with something. 'Your little games you were playing, showing me your tits like a slut, you never thought you'd be the one under my power, did you? You thought you'd have me.'

He took her tit and twisted it, his big fingers dwarfing her swollen nipple. This was a punishment Jenna had often dealt to her slaves and was shocked to find how much she liked being on the other end of it. The pain started small and grew so big she had to cry out.

'You're soaking. What a dirty little slut you are.

Pretending to be a dom, but you were gagging for this all the time.'

His light slaps travelled down her body, smacks raining down on her tits, belly and lower abdomen. Alexander pressed with the base of his hand on her bladder. It was full and Jenna winced. His eyes widened with cruel hope. Oh no, please not that, thought Jenna as he pressed harder. Watersports were her one taboo, the only punishment she'd never dished out to even her most depraved slaves. She shook her head.

'Poor you, you must be so thirsty, all this running around. Have a glass of water.' Jenna tried to refuse it but Alexander held her nose and forced it down her neck. The water was freezing as it cascaded over her breasts and belly.

'It will take a while for that water to pass through you,' he said. 'In the meantime, I intend to tease you a little more. You like to tease, don't you? Let's see if you can bear to receive what you so readily give.' Jenna thought that he would tickle or touch her but his version of teasing was much worse than that – it was showing her his body but not allowing her to touch it. He began to disrobe, slowly but precisely with none of the lingering delight of the true stripper. He removed his shoes and balled up the fine Scottish wool socks inside them. Then he took off his suit and trousers, and brushed them down before hanging them on a padded hanger on the back of his door. He did all of this without looking at her. Broad and muscular legs rose from the floor to meet a firm round butt encased in crisp white boxers. His tie was next, the pin removed first, then the tie itself. Finally he unbuttoned his shirt to reveal that perfectly sculpted torso and flat stomach with its maddeningly erotic scribble of hair beginning at his navel and shooting down underneath his boxers. This sight drove Jenna wild. He flipped through the pages of the *Financial Times*, still not looking at her. His shirt he placed over the back of his chair. Alexander had his back to Jenna as he rolled the white shorts over his manly hips. She wanted to cry out, 'Please let me see you,' but her pride forbade it.

She writhed on the floor, her poor body tender from the playsuit, her bladder growing more uncomfortably full by the second, her hands bound behind her back. Suddenly he was standing over her. His smooth balls and proud dick protruded and his face looked down on her like a cruel god. In his manicured hand he brandished a solid silver letter-opener in the shape of a dagger, an expensive office item which Jenna knew was as sharp as a razorblade. She shuddered, wondering what he wanted to do with it.

He bent down, slid the cold silver blade between Jenna's body and her tight leather bonds, making it even tighter for a second before twisting the blade and slashing at the expensive garment. The relief when the bonds were loosened was as great as an orgasm.

Alexander let her lie in the slashed black and scarlet strips of leather, before kneeling down so that his cock was jabbing at her tits. He poked her with his hard-on, using it to stroke her. It was such a soft touch and so at odds with his harsh words that she was ashamed of how grateful she felt.

'You like to think of yourself as a prick tease,' he said with a superior snarl. 'Well, I'm teasing you with a prick now, and you love it, don't you?'

Jenna could only nod in feeble agreement as he continued to stroke her whole body with the tip of his erect penis, his length tracing the red welts the harness had made all over her. It was a soft and gentle caress that contrasted with his utter domination of her and Jenna found it hugely sexy. His cock ran a line down between her breasts, pausing only to lightly smack against each nipple. Jenna watched as the treacherous tits swelled and darkened.

He knelt at her feet, forced her legs apart.

'You're dripping wet,' he said, scorn in his voice. 'I can't have that.'

He pulled a monogrammed handkerchief from his desk drawer, and used it to wipe Jenna's pussy dry. The handkerchief was sodden within seconds but she was still wet so he used another and then she was bone dry. As if on an impulse, he glanced down at the stained cotton in his hand, balled it up and stuffed it in Jenna's mouth.

She was just dry enough for his penetration of her lips to be slightly uncomfortable. His prick was finally in her and she was so grateful that she didn't care how much he had to humiliate her to do it. He fucked her and fucked her, placing one hand on her lower abdomen as the other worked her clitoris. She knew she was going to come and she knew what relaxing and abandoning herself to the spasms of orgasm would mean but she was so far gone she didn't care. Jenna felt heat sting her chest and cheeks as the climax welled up in her like a bubbling pan of water boiling over. She closed her eyes as she let go, relief flooding her entire frame, emptying her bladder as the convulsions rocked her body and heat prickled her skin. The sight of her water washing over his cock and balls made Alexander come too and he spunked inside her, his thick sticky white sperm mixing with her golden liquid. She closed her eyes again, lay there, gratified but debased, in a cooling pool of piss and spunk, listening to the sound of Alexander putting his clothes back on again. Shame, relief and pleasure raced around Jenna's mind, and only when he was gone did she open her eyes, struggle to her feet and wipe herself clean.

As Jenna cleaned up the office and looked down at

her tender flesh, she struggled to come to terms with what had just happened. The mistress had let herself become enslaved, humiliated and debased. The hunter was now the prey. Oh, and she had just experienced the best, most intense orgasm of her life.

CHAPTER NINE

'You let him do *what* to you?' Jacqueline was so shocked she froze with her fork halfway to her mouth, but Karl couldn't control his laughter.

'Now do you believe what I say about people going both ways?' he said, the ghost of a smug smile on his lips. Jenna sighed.

'I do and I don't,' she replied. 'No-one was more surprised than me when I loved it, but it's turned everything I know on its head. And it doesn't make me want to be his slave full time: it makes me want to dom him all the more. I need to redress the balance.'

Karl and Jacqueline pondered Jenna's problem, staring into their coffees.

'OK, so he didn't cure you of your dominant side,' said Jacqueline. 'That's OK. It just means you'll have to work smarter, not harder.'

'What do you mean?' asked Jenna.

'Well, you've been coming on really strong. That

doesn't work. He just says no and walks off. We need to be a bit more subtle.'

Jenna was intrigued.

'Go on . . .'

'Well . . .' said Jacqueline. 'What if we dress you as a sub or something so that he thinks he's got control – but really it's you who's calling the shots? If you surprise him in public then he won't be able to get away from you. It will be like Sydney all over again.'

'Jacqueline, you're a genius,' said Jenna, clapping her hands with excitement.

'I'm not just a pretty face,' replied Jacqueline.

'No, you're a great little cunt as well,' said Karl, reaching in and giving Jacqueline a long, tender, exploratory kiss. Jenna realised for the first time that her friends' relationship had grown deep and serious while she was absorbed with work and Alexander. She felt a stab of jealousy for the closeness they shared.

After lunch Jenna went straight back to the office and looked over Alexander's diary. She didn't have to thumb through many pages to find an appointment that would be perfect for her to exploit. She put in a call to Jacqueline, outlined her daring idea.

'I can't do it alone, Jacks,' she told her friend. 'Will you help me out?'

'I think you're absolutely insane,' said Jacqueline.

'But you'll help me anyway,' Jenna ordered.

'Oh yes.'

Town planning applications aren't usually the kind of thing to send a sexual frisson through a girl, but Alexander was debating a controversial new development live on television and Jenna couldn't think of a better opportunity to carry out her plan to teach Alexander who was boss once and for all.

The debate was taking place in a town hall in the grotty suburb of South London that was Alexander's constituency. Jenna was grateful she'd never had to visit it before. She was there at eight o'clock, clipboard in hand, Jacqueline posing as her PA, the pair ostensibly running security checks but really sizing up the venue, working out a way to put her plan into action. When she saw the lectern Alexander would be speaking from – raised on a podium, made of curved walnut panelling which hid the speaker's lower body from view – she said a silent prayer of thanks.

Jenna and Jacqueline had had to seize their moment when the camera crew broke for tea. Jenna disrobed behind a curtain on the stage, swapping her clothes for a length of coarse fisherman's rope.

'It's weird, me tying you up rather than the other way

round,' said Jacqueline, as she arranged a length of rope so that it bisected Jenna's breast at the nipple, sending a half-melon of flesh spilling out above and below the bondage. Jenna spread her legs and Jacqueline deftly threaded the rope through, parting Jenna's cunt so that it brushed her clitoris.

'Is it doing anything for you?' asked Jenna, intrigued, as Jacqueline fastened her hands on her lap and completed her work with a large, chunky granny-knot that Jenna would never be able to undo on her own.

'Not really,' confessed Jacqueline. 'I don't care what Karl says, I'm a sub through and through. You look stunning though. He'll be rock-hard in your mouth.'

Jacqueline laid a bottle of water on its side on a ledge inside the lectern so that Jenna would be able to drink from it, like a hamster in a cage. For what she had in mind, she would need a limber, wet mouth. She heard Jacqueline's footsteps retreating across the stage and felt the temperature in the room rise, a hot, dry heat as the lights and cameras were turned on and people began to file into the hall.

At the sound of voices, Jenna felt her pulse begin to quicken at her neck as well as between her legs, and her thighs, stuck together, were damp with sweat and her juices. She began to shiver with excitement as a familiar pair of long legs, dressed in light wool trousers with a sharp crease down the front, stood in front of the lectern where she crouched. She wanted to touch him now, but forced herself to wait.

Alexander and his opponent were introduced and both made their opening speeches. He sounded masterful and full of confidence – arrogance, even – but his left toe, hidden from view of the pubic, tapped furiously, a sign of vulnerability that empowered Jenna. Once or twice, he banged his fist on the lectern to make a point. Jenna shuddered with desire as the vibrations travelled through her bound body.

Jenna edged forward on her knees and used her teeth to pull back the curtain. Alexander glanced down at the sight before him – his beautiful bronzed assistant, voluntarily wound around with rope that squeezed her firm breasts and made her powerless, knelt before him in a position of absolute submission, but the expression on her face was anything but meek and mild. He was momentarily and uncharacteristically struck dumb.

Jenna pushed her tits against his legs and licked her lips. Then she leaned in and breathed softly on his crotch, knowing the warm air from her mouth would heat up his prick. To her delight, he started getting hard. She saw the bulge form in his trousers, lifting up the flap of his waistcoat, and protrude against his right thigh. Jenna bared her teeth and used them to undo the buttons of his fly, grateful for the rope which chafed at her breasts and roughly caressed her clit. She was pleased and turned on to notice that Alexander had gone without his crisp white boxers. The long, pink shaft of his cock bobbed free and grew before her eyes, hidden from view of the cameras and everyone in the hall, but gloriously visible to Jenna. She closed her lips and held them against the tip of his prick. To taste him after all this time was heaven. She kept her mouth closed as she bore down on his penis, knowing that penetrating this make-believe resistance would send his arousal through the roof. The whole of his right leg now shook uncontrollably, although his voice remained steady with a quaver imperceptible to all but her.

Jenna might be dressed as a sub, but she was the one with all the power here. She looked up at Alexander's face, impressed that he was managing to control himself above the waist. She was acutely aware of her own frustration as she lavished all her attention on Alexander, her tongue swirling over the sensitive head of his erection, knowing that he wouldn't be able to resist it, wishing it was his tongue on her clit. This thought made her intensify her own ministrations and she sucked hard, triggering the climax he was powerless to resist. He managed to disguise his orgasm as a coughing fit, his hips thrusting forwards, about to pump Jenna's mouth full of spunk. She jerked her head back so that his prick was shooting into the air, his milk decorating her whole body. He looked down at her, covered in cum, aghast at what had just happened.

Jenna winked at him, and used her tongue and teeth to zip him up again. The debate carried on, Alexander winning over the crowd with his usual mixture of wit and élan. Jenna watched as he left the press conference. The look he gave her before leaving was the sternest she had ever been on the receiving end of. It was a cruel, merciless glare which both terrified and exhilarated her.

Once the press and public had filed out, Jacqueline crept back to the place where she had left Jenna, who untied her.

'Christ, that was hot,' said Jenna, stretching out aching limbs which were criss-crossed with red-raw rope burns.

'That was horny,' said Jacqueline. 'Knowing you were sucking him off . . . he was helpless between your lips.' Then, shyly, 'I was jealous.' Jenna knew Jacqueline well enough by now to know when she was fishing for punishment.

'Come on then,' said Jenna, shrugging off her ropes. 'Clean me up.' Jacqueline began to tongue-bathe Jenna, sucking Alexander's spunk off her skin and soothing her fiery flesh. When the smaller woman's efforts had completely cleansed her of any droplets of spunk, Jenna spread her legs to reveal a swollen, yearning clit. 'Did I say you could finish?' asked Jenna, an eyebrow arched. Jacqueline dropped to her knees, and let her tongue and lips flutter over Jenna's bud in the quick-fire caresses she knew her mistress loved. Jenna came hard, a gush of juice hot and wet between her legs.

'Now then,' she said, businesslike and brisk now that her climax was over, as Jacqueline handed over her clothes. 'I'd better go and face the music.'

Alexander was waiting for her at the office, towering over his desk, hands balled into fists. She had never seen him look this angry, or this sexy.

'Something wrong?' she asked him.

'You know fucking well what's wrong.' He spoke in the stage whisper of someone who is seconds away from losing his temper and roaring with rage. 'You stupid, arrogant little bitch. How dare you jeopardise my career like that? How dare you?'

'You fucking loved it,' said Jenna. 'You came so hard you were shaking. Why can't you admit it? You're a fucking prick.'

'And you're fucking fired.' Now it was Jenna's turn to feel white-hot anger burning in her belly. How dare he apply these double standards to their relationship?

'You can't fire me,' Jenna shot back. 'Because I quit.'

'Fine!' shouted Alexander, and turned his back to her. Jenna saw that he was shaking. Strong words were on the tip of her tongue: she was about to let rip, telling him that he was a bully but a coward too, afraid to let

a strong woman take control of him, terrified to admit
that he liked it. But she reconsidered and bit the words
back before they were spoken. Inspiration struck her
and she decided to try a different tactic. She walked
around the desk and placed a hand on Alexander's trembling shoulder.

'Let it go,' she said, tenderly. 'Let me take charge. I
give you my permission, and my promise. You're safe with
me. Trust me. Abandon yourself to me.'

Jenna's gentle words had the effect she had been after.
Alexander's shoulders relaxed, his breathing grew softer
and his body ceased to shudder. Gently, Jenna reached
around his body and unbuckled his trousers. Her hand
closed on a proud hard-on, and she ran her fingers up
and down the length of it.

'Let me take control,' she whispered in his ear. 'Give
in to me.'

His cock grew in her hand, and as the balance of
power finally transferred in her favour, Jenna found that
it was her turn to shake with desire and anticipation. A
warm wet pulse began to hammer between her legs and
she felt her nipples grow hard.

'OK,' she said, her voice still barely audible. 'Good
boy. Well done. Now, I want you to slip these trousers
over your hips and bend over your desk. Will you do that
for me?'

To Jenna's delight, Alexander nodded his head eagerly. She took a step back, watching as he took down his trousers. The ass that was now bent over the desk was toned and defined, smooth and solid with a light smattering of brown hair at the base of the spine. Jenna felt her pussy begin to spasm.

'Right then,' she said, her voice growing louder and more strident. 'You're playing by my rules now. And the first thing I need to do is break you in.'

She got Alexander to spit on her fingers and inserted them one by one into his tight ass hole, teasing his body from the inside out. The more mercilessly she explored him, the more excited they both grew: Alexander was as hard as Jenna was wet, and she was soon in full dominatrix mode. When he began begging for mercy, she let rip.

'Turn over,' she said. 'You pathetic, dirty bastard.' He lay back on his desk, his dick bigger than Jenna had ever seen it, standing proudly up to his navel. Pre-cum glistened on the tip. Jenna decided to punish him for that.

'Can't you control yourself? This is for what happened yesterday.' She slapped him hard across the face. His dick got bigger. 'This is for not having the balls to admit what you like.' Another slap, this time across his balls. 'And this,' said Jenna, shoving the fingers that had been up his ass into his slack mouth, 'is for making me wait five fucking years before getting you where I want you.' She had finally dealt out enough humiliation for him to be hard. Taking his fat cock in her hand, she brutally squeezed a couple of times to let him know who was boss before shoving it into her greedy wet hole. It filled her up more completely than she had ever thought possible, and his face when he came, that vulnerable, little-boy look that she had seen in Sydney, made her feel like the queen of the world. She took his fingers, rubbed them over her pulsating clit and climaxed before collapsing onto his prone body.

The two of them lay on the desk, Alexander on his back with his feet on the floor, Jenna loosely slumped over him, while his dick received the spontaneous squeezes of Jenna's post-orgasm pussy. Then, and only then, did they kiss, a deep and tender meeting of mouths that negated the need for apologies or explanations.

'Jenna,' said Alexander, his hand fishing down her top and finding her breast, cupping it with a large, masculine hand. It was the first time he had addressed her by her name in nearly two months of employing her.

'What is it, you dirty bastard?' said Jenna, running her fingers through the hair on the nape of his neck and pulling it back hard so that he was forced to look her in the eye. He cleared his throat before continuing. 'Jenna,' he said, his immaculate English vowels sexier than ever now that they were hoarse and husky. 'Would you like your job back?'

CHAPTER TEN

Jenna watched the live broadcast of Alexander's speech from the monitor in their new office, making notes with her right hand and idly stroking her clitoris with her left. Pride and lust flooded through her as he spoke the words that they had drafted together the evening before, in a late-night working session which had culminated in a three-page speech being written and Alexander binding Jenna's wrists together with his silk tie before inserting a double-headed vibrator in her cunt and ass and masturbating over her face. The silk tie, which Jenna's struggles had stretched and warped until it was unwearable, was currently knotted around the top of Jenna's left thigh. She licked her lips at the memory, and tried to concentrate on Alexander's ad-libs as his sharp tongue was turned on his political opponents.

In the three months since she had crawled underneath that podium and wrapped her lips around Alexander's cock, her career and her relationship had both soared. At work, they were an unstoppable force, Alexander tipped to be the country's youngest minister thanks in no small part to his dynamic head of research.

In bed, they had only one rule: that they took it in turns to be each other's slave. This strictly observed system of alternation had been a mutual idea and a stroke of genius. No matter how domineering either of them felt, they could not take control unless it was their turn to do so: Jenna relished this rule as it gave her permission to yield even when she thought she didn't want to. Under Alexander's command, Jenna had found herself astonishingly compliant: with multiple orgasms as her prize, she found that she welcomed every humiliation he could bestow upon her. And, once she had broken down his initial reluctance to accept her as his mistress, she was astonished by Alexander's capacity for subservience. Devising new and original punishments was as challenging as any professional task he ever set her. He was not the straightforward sub she had expected him to be – and she loved him all the more for it.

As the sun set over London, Alexander lay prone on the floor of Jenna's apartment, his legs forced apart by a black chrome bar that was shackled to his ankles and his arms splayed by a similar contraption which attached to his wrists and his neck. He bit down hard on the riding crop which had been forced between his teeth. Jenna, wearing one of Alexander's crisp white shirts, unbuttoned to display firm breasts with erect nipples, straddled his body, powering down with her thighs, hooking her forefingers between her fat pussy lips and parting them slightly to show him the swelling of her clitoris and the shiny pink shell of her cunt, slick with her juices.

'Mfnffmm, nmmm, nnnnffnf,' said Alexander, the vein that bulged on his neck matching the one that snaked along the shaft of his turgid dick.

'What's that, slave?' said Jenna, cupping her hand behind her ear. 'Did you want something?'

Alexander struggled, the muscles on his arms and chest rippling as he struggled to break free of his irons. He tried to rid his mouth of the crop, but Jenna had fastened the neck brace so tightly that he could not move his jaw.

'Did you want, for example, for me to wrap my tight hole around your prick? Hmm? Is that what you're trying to tell me?' She remained in a squatting position, her glistening cunt a hair's breadth away from the smooth tip of Alexander's prick. She adjusted the cufflinks mono-grammed with Alexander's initials that glittered at her wrists and examined her nails. He squirmed beneath her, his muffled moans growing louder.

'I'm sorry, I can't hear you,' Jenna said, lowering herself a fraction of a centimetre so that she could feel the warmth of his body but not make contact with his skin. She frowned. 'What have I told you about mumbling to me?'

She delivered a sharp slap to the side of Alexander's face. His dick, already fat and solid, became even more engorged. His cock rose to meet her cunt. Jenna closed her own eyes and sighed. She had intended to punish Alexander if he had made first contact but when his flesh brushed against hers, she surrendered to its magnetism. She let her thighs go slack and her pussy, already convulsing with pre-orgasmic contractions, was let down onto Alexander's waiting prick, wrapping itself around the warm rod of flesh. She let the rough scrawl of his pubic hair massage her proudly stiff clitoris. She came in seconds, knowing that Alexander's climax would not be far behind. Jenna felt his balls brush her ass as they rose up into his body, then clamped her thumb and forefinger over his nose, denying him breath for a split second before he came. His eyes widened as pleasure merged with panic, before Jenna released her grip. Oxygen flooded Alexander's lungs at the same time as his spunk filled Jenna's hole, and she tightened her tender pussy around his grateful cock, ripping the crop from his mouth so that he could thank her for his climax. As soon as he began to speak, she bent down to kiss the words from his lips, her breasts brushing against the firm torso that was slick with sweat, hands unfastening the neck brace, her fingers stroking the hair of the man who was her employer, her lover, her slave.

Ten minutes later they were in Jenna's shower, their two bodies wedged into a cubicle designed for one.

'My turn next time,' said Alexander, working the shampoo into Jenna's hair, taking care not to let any suds sting her eyes.

'I know,' said Jenna, enjoying his fingers massaging her scalp. 'I can't wait to find out what you've got planned.' She let the water cascade over her body, washing her clean. She used a sponge to bathe the red welts on Alexander's neck. 'I do hope your collar and tie cover that mark,' she said, kissing him better as he turned off the water. 'We can't have you looking like a sub in front of the voters, can we?'

They dried each other, Jenna astonished to find, as he threaded a soft white towel through her legs and sawed at her clit, that she was ready to make love again. The flutter between her thighs became a throb. She glanced down at Alexander's dick, still in recovery, wondering if he was ready for round two.

'I know that look,' he said, as she licked her lips and turned her face up towards his. 'Christ, you really are an insatiable little slut, aren't you.'

Jenna didn't answer, but instead pulled him to her, their two bodies coming together as equals, their kisses tender rather than sparring, as they took the first steps towards the 'straight' sex that Jenna would once have dismissed as vanilla but she now found almost as rewarding as power play. As Alexander's hands smoothed down the damp skin on her butt and back and his dick stiffened against her thigh, she felt her insides turn into hot liquid and her pussy soften and yield. He was inside her in seconds, lifting her up effortlessly, staggering forwards with her still impaled on his cock, her tits squashed up against his chest. With a cold slap, she felt the tiled wall on her wet back and leaned against it as Alexander gently rocked her to orgasm. He came inside her, copious spunk gushing forth from balls she thought she'd drained less than an hour ago. When they had both come, they slid down the wall together, slumped together on white towels strewn on the floor.

'There's just one thing I don't know,' said Jenna, as Alexander's tongue played join-the-dots with the tiny nicks and bruises that now dappled Jenna's skin. 'What took you so long? To let me take charge.' Her hand cupped his still-sensitive balls and made him wince.

'Let me explain something, Jenna,' said Alexander, turning over onto his belly and propping himself up on his meaty forearms. 'Ever since I was a boy, I'd been obsessed with politics and power. It was all I wanted, from school onwards. And I found it so easy to control people. Colleagues, women, friends, . . . no-one had ever challenged me. And then you came skating round the corner in Sydney, and told me what to do, and it was the most intense orgasm I'd ever had. Afterwards, I was terrified. I was scared of what would happen if I let my guard down again. I was so relieved that you were on the other side of the world, that you were a one-off.' He bit down on Jenna's breast as if to assert his dominance while explaining his vulnerability. 'And then you turned up here, in my office, and now I had a proper career and everything to lose . . . you can see why I was scared.'

'So that's why you had to dominate me before you'd let me take charge of you,' replied Jenna, sure she had solved the final mystery of Alexander's mind game. 'You needed to know that I could be vulnerable too before we could take things further. That's so sweet.'

'No,' said Alexander, hooking a finger inside Jenna's cunt and massaging their mingled juices into her. He laughed at her. 'It's a nice theory, but the truth is much less complicated.'

'What then?' said Jenna.

'It was my turn,' he said, smiling. Jenna joined in his laughter, then felt a churning sensation overwhelm her body as Alexander's eyes grew serious. 'And it's my turn again now. Close your eyes.'

Jenna let her eyelids lower and fall. Let the surrender begin.

True Passion:
A Tale of Desire as Told
to Madame B

Bold sexual adventurer Katie reveals her innermost secrets to our mysterious hostess, Madame B, and tells a tale of seduction and fantasies made real. She falls for the charms of older man Alex, and makes it her mission (and his) to experience every thrill life has to offer.

As Katie pushes their passion to extremes, will Alex surrender to her every whim? *True Passion* tells their scintillating story, and ensures that nothing remains a secret any more.

ISBN: 9780091924881

£6.99

Too Hot to Handle:
More True Stories
from Madame B

Our mysterious hostess Madame B tells the tales of ten young women who have pushed passion to the very limit. Delicious desires and sexy secrets are revealed, with steamy scenarios and extreme indulgences stripped bare.

Includes:

Executive Decision – It's the career chance of a lifetime. PA to a gorgeous, jet-setting executive. Amanda wants the job – and him – so badly. Then he asks if she has any 'extra services' to offer.

Coming Up Roses – Kara can't face a day in the office and calls in sick. That's when she notices two gardeners working outside. It's hot, they're sweating. So Kara invites them both in for a shower . . .

Double Fantasy – Identical twins Gilly and Annie secretly share their men. So when fit delivery guy Rob turns up with a washing machine, Gilly has her fun on top of it – and then lets Annie take over.

Tunnel Vision – She spots him at check-in, and he's sitting opposite her in first class. He passes her a mobile number. She texts. He texts. And things get steamy.

Backstage Pass – Everyone knows him, the rock star who regularly tops the charts. Ali just has to have him, and blags a backstage pass . . .

ISBN: 9780091924966
£6.99

Available now at www.rbooks.co.uk

Lost in Lust:
More Tales
from Madame B

Madame B is back, with ten more sexy tales from women who do the things you secretly want to do – but would never dare.

Includes:

Hire Love – Hannah hires a male escort for a high-powered work party, but it turns into more than a simple business transaction.

The Mistress's Apprentice – Tina discovers how thrilling power can be when she finds herself working in a place where submission and domination are all in a day's work.

The Hitcher – Alice and Paul's erotic encounter with a young hitch-hiker turns into the ride of a lifetime.

Window Shopping – a shared fantasy of sex in public is made real when Bethany and Max take a big risk . . .

El Ritmo del Noche – at a fiesta on holiday in Spain, Helen finds out that even the prissiest English girl needs a little Latin in her.

ISBN: 9780091916480

£6.99

Available now at www.rbooks.co.uk